Danger in the Streets

"Look at this mess," Joe said, kicking at a piece of paper that had blown onto the sidewalk. The street was littered with colorful flyers.

Jake picked up a flyer, held it up, and read, " 'Take Back Our Streets.' Hmmph."

"Looks like the councilwoman's people don't know how to pick up after themselves," Frank said.

The group reached the corner and was waiting for the walk signal.

When the light changed the sound of a racing car engine shattered the stillness of the night air.

Joe looked up just in time to see a red sport utility vehicle with no headlights on speeding straight at them.

"Look out!" he cried.

The Hardy Boys Mystery Stories

Available from MINSTREL Books

THE HARDY BOYS®

163

THE SPY THAT NEVER LIES

FRANKLIN W. DIXON

A MINSTREL® BOOK

Published by POCKET BOOKS
New York   London   Toronto   Sydney   Singapore

This book is a work of fiction. Names, characters, places and incidents are products of the author's imagination or are used fictitiously. Any resemblance to actual events or locales or persons, living or dead, is entirely coincidental.

A MINSTREL PAPERBACK *Original*

A Minstrel Book published by
POCKET BOOKS, a division of Simon & Schuster, Inc.
1230 Avenue of the Americas, New York, NY 10020

Copyright © 2000 by Simon & Schuster, Inc.

Front cover illustration by Jeff Walker

ISBN: 0-671-04760-4

First Minstrel Books printing September 2000

10 9 8 7 6 5 4 3 2 1

Printed in the U.S.A.

Contents

THE SPY THAT NEVER LIES

1 Take Back Our Streets

"Move along, you kids," the police officer said. His tone wasn't the friendliest as he looked straight at Frank and Joe Hardy and their friend Jamal Hawkins. The three teens were standing outside Java John's, a coffee shop in downtown Bayport.

Seventeen-year-old Joe, the younger of the brothers, bristled a bit, his blue eyes flashing. "We aren't doing anything wrong," Joe protested. "We're just standing here."

"We're waiting for some friends," Jamal put in.

"Well, wait somewhere else," the officer said. "We've got a march coming through here soon, and we don't want any trouble."

"What kind of a march, Officer Sullivan?" Frank

Hardy asked. He had read the police officer's name from his name tag.

"Councilwoman Hamilton's Take Back Our Streets march and rally. Don't you kids read the papers?"

Thinking about it, Frank did remember seeing a story about the rally in the Bayport *Times*. The councilwoman was on a crusade against crime and had planned this march to publicize it.

"I didn't know that we'd lost the streets," Jamal said, a smile creasing his handsome face.

Officer Sullivan scowled. "Just move along, wiseguy," he said. "We've had enough trouble with you teens lately."

Frank could see both Joe and Jamal clench their teeth at the implication. Eighteen-year-old Frank quickly stepped in front of his brother and their friend.

"Come on, guys," he said, gently nudging them backward. "We can wait inside the coffee shop."

Joe and Jamal nodded, and the three of them headed for the door. The officer turned and walked away down the street.

"Must be going to annoy someone else," Joe muttered.

"Chill, Joe," Frank said. "He was just doing his job."

"I'm with Joe," Jamal said. "I don't think his job is to hassle us."

"I don't think he was worried about *us*," Frank

said, "not in particular anyway. There has been a lot of trouble with teen vandalism in this part of town lately." He stepped inside Java John's.

"I know that," Joe said, following his older brother inside. "But the police shouldn't be razzing us just because of some other teens."

Jamal, right behind Joe, shrugged. "Sometimes it's hard to tell the good guys from the bad guys, I guess." He motioned to a table near the big window facing the street. "We should be able to spot Jake and Vanessa from there. They should be here any minute."

The Hardys nodded their agreement, and all three sat down. When the waitress came, they all ordered coffee.

"How long have you known Jake Martins, Jamal?" Frank asked.

"Just over a year," Jamal replied. "He did some computer work for my dad's company last summer and continued working some after school started. We hung out and got to be friends. He's a freshman at the Bayport Institute of Technology."

"That's just down the street, isn't it?" Joe said as their coffees arrived.

Jamal nodded and took a sip of his drink. "Yeah. It's not too far. That's why we chose this spot to meet. Jake doesn't have a car—he walks everywhere."

"Fitness nut?" Frank asked.

Jamal laughed. "Far from it. Just strapped for cash, like most college students."

"And you think he's in trouble?" Joe asked.

"I wouldn't say *trouble*," Jamal said, "but there's definitely something funny going on with him. He quit his job with my dad's company and took a new one. He's canceled out on me a couple of times when we were supposed to do stuff together—like go to a computer game convention—without any good reason."

"Maybe he's just busy," Joe said.

"That's what I thought at first, since he's a freshman in college. But that's not the only thing. He's gotten moody and withdrawn. He doesn't look well, either. His parents moved out of town before the semester started, so . . ."

Joe nodded. "You think he doesn't have anyone to talk to."

"It's not just that," Jamal said. "He doesn't seem to *want* to talk to anyone. Jake won't tell me or anybody else what's going on. My dad checked with his parents and they think everything's okay. But I'm worried about him. I thought maybe you guys could help me find out what's bugging him."

Joe leaned back in his chair. "How the mighty have fallen," he said. "From top-flight detectives to advice givers for lonely college students."

Frank chuckled. "This Vanessa you mentioned," he

said to Jamal, "who is she? How does Jake know her?"

"Her name is Vanessa Robinson," Jamal said. "The two of them work together, and I think they're in some of the same classes at BIT. I saw her at one of the college volleyball games, but we never got a chance to talk. Jake mentioned that he knew her. I told him that I wanted to meet her and asked him to bring her along this evening. It was the only way I could think of to lure him out of his apartment."

"So, she's just a smoke screen for us to meet Jake?" Frank asked.

Joe laughed. "Frank, I've seen this girl. She used to compete in a volleyball league against Iola." Iola Morton was Joe's girlfriend. "I suspect there's more to Jamal's story than he's letting on."

Jamal's chestnut brown face reddened a bit. "Okay," he said, "I admit I want to meet her. But I'm really concerned about Jake, too."

Frank smiled. "So you decided to kill two birds with one stone."

"Why not?" Jamal asked, shrugging. "There's no law against a guy meeting a new girl while helping out a friend."

Frank and Joe chuckled. Then something outside the window caught Joe's eye.

"Isn't that Vince Morelli?" Frank asked, indicating one of two guys walking past the coffee shop.

"Yeah," Jamal said. "And that's Jay Stone with him. What are they up to?"

Morelli was tall and built like a prize fighter; Stone was shorter and rail thin. Both teens had the word *Kings* painted in red and yellow letters on the backs of their black leather jackets. They glanced around suspiciously as they walked.

"Up to no good, if I know anything about the two of them," Joe said. "They're the ones the council-woman should be cracking down on, not us. Maybe we should follow them, see what's going on."

"No time, Joe," Jamal replied. "Here are Jake and Vanessa now." He stood and waved to the pair as they entered the coffee shop. "Hey, Jake! Over here!"

The Hardys sized up the two people coming toward them. Jake Martins was a bit shorter than Jamal, and nowhere near as athletic looking. He had scraggly brown hair and a bit of a beard on his chin, and was wearing torn blue jeans and a BIT T-shirt. He was pale and looked worn out, but he waved back to Jamal with some enthusiasm.

The young woman with him was tall, thin, and moved with the easy grace of an athlete. Over her red dress she was wearing a black satin jacket with the word *Securitech* printed on the breast pocket.

She had deep brown skin and short black hair. Her dark eyes sparkled as she smiled at the group.

Jamal and the Hardys stood up as Jake and Vanessa approached the table. "Hey, Jake, good to see you," Jamal greeted his friend. Then he turned to the young woman and extended his hand. "You must be Vanessa. I'm Jamal Hawkins, and these are my friends Frank and Joe Hardy. Frank's the brunette, Joe's the blond."

"Vanessa Robinson," she said, shaking Jamal's hand, then Joe's, and finally Frank's. "Pleased to meet you all. Jake's told me quite a bit about you, Jamal."

"Not too much, I hope," Jamal said, smiling.

While Jamal flagged the waitress so that the newcomers could order, Jake shook hands with the Hardys. "Pleased to meet you," he said. "Jacob Martins. My friends call me Jake." Frank and Joe both noticed that although his greeting was warm, his hand was clammy.

"Did you walk here?" Joe asked.

"Sure," Jake said. "It's not that far, and besides, I don't own a car."

"You'd think he'd be in better shape," Vanessa said jokingly, "considering he walks everywhere."

"Hey," Jake said, "not everyone is a born athlete, like you and Jamal." He turned to the Hardys and asked, "Are you two into sports?"

"Some football," Joe said.

"Some baseball," Frank added.

7

Jamal laughed. "Don't let the two of them fool you, Jake," he said. "Both of them have natural talent."

Jake leaned back in his chair. "Looks like I'm the only intellectual in the group, then," he said kiddingly.

The waitress returned with Jake's and Vanessa's orders, and the conversation paused a moment as the five teens sipped their coffees. Through the window they could see a huge group of people moving rapidly down the street.

"What's that about?" Vanessa asked.

"Must be the Take Back Our Streets march and rally," Joe said. "What a crowd."

"I didn't know any of our streets were missing," Vanessa quipped.

Jamal laughed. "That's what I said, too."

"Looks like a pretty big deal," Frank said, craning his neck to get a better view. "I see a bunch of TV cameras. Councilwoman Hamilton sure knows how to draw a crowd."

"She's been riding our boss at work pretty hard, too," Jake said.

"Oh, yeah? Where do you work, Jake?" Joe asked.

"Vanessa and I both work at Securitech. It's the high-tech surveillance company working on the college's and the city's new security system."

"Is that the company that's been installing cameras on light poles all around town?" Frank asked.

"That's it," Vanessa said. "We've been"—she hesitated a moment before continuing—"working with the city on it."

The Hardys noticed that both Vanessa and Jake seemed a bit uncomfortable about discussing their jobs. Jamal noticed it, too. "Is there some kind of trouble at work?" he asked.

Jake shook his head. "No. Nothing. It's just that what we're doing is pretty secret. We're not supposed to talk about it."

"There's a big announcement on campus tomorrow for the media, if you want to find out about it," Vanessa said. "A lot of us who worked on the project will be there."

"We'll come. No school tomorrow," Jamal said.

Jake put his head in his hands and ran his fingers through his curly brown hair. "Oh, man," he said. "I'd almost forgotten about that press conference. I've got to get going. I still have a lot of work to do tonight." He put some money on the table for the bill, then jumped up.

"I've got stuff to do, too," Vanessa said, getting up. "It was nice meeting all of you."

Jamal and the Hardys got to their feet. "Hey, I could give you a lift home, if you like," Jamal said to Vanessa.

"Great," Vanessa said. "I'm in a dorm on campus."

9

Frank put some more money on the table to cover their bill and tip.

"Where are you headed, Jake?" Joe asked. "Want a lift?"

"I could use one, thanks," Jake said. "I've got a place off campus. They ran out of dorm space before I got my housing application in."

"That's our Jake," Vanessa said. "He'd forget his head if it weren't nailed to his shoulders."

"It's not the best place," Jake said defensively, "but at least it's cheap."

With Jamal leading the way, they exited Java John's. "I'm parked just around the block," he said.

"We're that way, too," Frank added. It had gotten dark while they were inside, and the street was pretty much deserted now. In the distance they could hear the rally still going strong.

"Look at this mess," Joe said, kicking at a piece of paper that had blown onto the sidewalk. The street was littered with colorful flyers.

Jake picked up a flyer, held it up, and read, " 'Take Back Our Streets.' Hmmph."

"Looks like the councilwoman's people don't know how to pick up after themselves," Frank said.

"Maybe we should start a new campaign—Clean Up Our Streets," Jamal suggested.

The group reached the corner and was waiting for the walk signal.

When the light changed the sound of a racing car engine shattered the stillness of the night air.

Joe looked up just in time to see a red sport utility vehicle with no headlights on speeding straight at them.

"Look out!" he cried.

2 A Near Miss

At the last second the SUV swerved away and came racing parallel to the curb, its brakes squealing loudly.

Vanessa and Jamal, who had just stepped off the curb, jumped back up to avoid being hit.

The window on the driver's side of the car slid down, and someone yelled, "Take back *this!*" A large object in a brown paper bag sailed out the open window. Joe and Frank ducked, but Jake wasn't as fast as the brothers.

The package hit him square in the forehead. He dropped the flyer he had been looking at and fell to his knees, his forehead bleeding from a one-inch gash. Joe and Frank ripped open the bag and saw that it contained a six-pack of empty soda bottles.

While Frank went to help Jake, Joe chased after the car. "Come back here!" the younger Hardy yelled as the car zoomed into the night. He ran behind it for two blocks but finally had to give up.

When Joe returned to the group, he found that Frank had already bandaged Jake's head with a handkerchief. Vanessa and Jamal hovered around their friend, looking concerned.

"You really should go to the hospital," Frank said to Jake. "A head wound like this can be worse than it looks."

Jake shook his head groggily. "No. I can't," he said. "I don't have time. I've got a paper to do, and . . ." He trailed off, and Frank had to support him for a moment.

Frank exchanged a worried glance with his brother. Clearly they both thought Jake should go to the hospital, but if he didn't want to go, they couldn't force him. Frank said, "Get anything on that car, Joe?"

"Nothing," Joe responded, shaking his head. "Just a red SUV like a million others. I couldn't see past the tinted windows, and the license plate was covered with mud."

"A sure sign of troublemakers," Frank said, somewhat exasperated.

"The only identifying mark I saw on the car was a Chaos Rules bumper sticker," Joe finished.

"You think the owner is an anarchist?" Vanessa asked.

"Maybe just a video game enthusiast," Frank said. "We worked on a case about the Chaos video game series a while back."

"The bumper sticker doesn't give us much to go on either way," Joe said.

"Maybe the councilwoman is right," Vanessa said. "Maybe this city *is* having a crime problem."

"We'll find out tomorrow, I guess," Jamal said. "She's going to be at the press conference, isn't she?"

Vanessa smiled at him. "You *did* read a paper once, didn't you?" she said jokingly. She turned from Jamal to her friend. "How are you feeling, Jake?"

"I've been better," Jake said.

"You're sure you don't want to go to the hospital?" Frank asked.

"No," Jake said. "Home will be fine. I've got a paper to finish for Firestein's computer programming class."

"He'd understand your turning the paper in late if you were in the hospital," Jamal said.

Vanessa rolled her eyes. "That ogre? Being dead isn't enough of an excuse for missing one of Firestein's classes. Never having been born—now, *that* might work for not turning in a paper."

"He's pretty tough, all right," Jake said. "I wish he wasn't. Bet you do, too, Vanessa."

"I don't much care at this point," Vanessa said.

"Don't forget, Jake, we're supposed to be at the press conference tomorrow, too. It's part of our job."

"Why is that?" Frank asked.

"Securitech wants to thank the people who worked on the project," Vanessa said. "A lot of the company's employees are students at BIT."

"Is that why they're holding the press conference on campus?" Joe asked.

"I think so," Jake said. "That and there's been some trouble with vandalism on campus. The new system should change that, though. Oops! Forget I said that. My head must really be ringing."

Vanessa smiled at him. "It's all been very hush-hush," she said. "But most of the details have been in the paper. Securitech is providing Bayport with a crime surveillance and prevention system. The cameras you mentioned are part of it."

Joe spotted a camera on a nearby light pole. "Well," he said, pointing toward it, "let's hope they caught that bottle-thrower on tape."

"Oh, the system hasn't been activated, yet," Vanessa said.

Joe snapped his fingers in frustration. "Just our luck."

"Guys," Jamal said, "Jake's looking a little woozy again."

"I'm okay," Jake said as Frank went to help him. "I just need to get home, that's all."

"Good idea," Frank said. He and Joe helped Jake around the corner and down the street to where the Hardys had parked their van.

Jamal led Vanessa in the other direction. "See you guys tomorrow," he said.

"Yes," Vanessa said. "Nice meeting both of you. Jake, call me and let me know if you're okay."

"Okay," Jake replied.

"And don't forget about tomorrow," she called over her shoulder.

"I won't," Jake said.

Vanessa and Jamal got into Jamal's sedan and drove off. The Hardys reached their van with Jake in tow.

"I'm really okay, you know," Jake said.

Frank and Joe glanced at Jake, then at each other.

"If you say so," Joe said.

"We'd feel better, though, if you'd let us take you to the hospital."

Jake shook his head and a pained expression came over his face. "No. I can't. I really have to work on my paper. I probably shouldn't even have come out tonight, but Jamal was pretty insistent."

"He can be that way," Joe said, smiling. He slid open the side door of the van. Jake got inside, seated himself, and buckled himself in. Frank got behind the wheel; Joe took the front passenger seat. They both buckled in, and Frank started the engine.

16

He turned to Jake and asked, "Where to?"

"Smith Street, near the corner of Lester," Jake said. He closed his eyes and leaned back in his seat. "Thanks for the lift, guys."

"It's the least we can do," Joe said.

"You said you were living off campus?" Frank said.

"Yeah," Jake replied. "It's a subsidized apartment just a few blocks from school. There's been a jump in enrollment at BIT in the last few years."

"Because of the computer boom, you mean," Joe said.

"Yes," Jake said. "The college ran out of dorm rooms, so they arranged for alternate housing off campus. Like I said, it's not the best place, but it's pretty close to my classes."

"You majoring in computer science, Jake?" Frank asked. He turned the van toward the campus and headed for Smith Street.

"Yeah," Jake said. "That's why Professor Firestein's class is so important to me. If I don't pass it, I'll have to take it again next year."

"How far?" Frank asked as he turned the car onto Smith Street.

"Just a couple of blocks," Jake said. "The number is Twenty-five Ten. It's a two-story yellow-brick apartment building."

"Gotcha," Frank said.

17

"So, between working at Securitech and school, I imagine you stay pretty busy," Joe said.

"Yeah," Jake said. "Too busy, sometimes." He sounded tired.

"What kind of work do you do?" Joe asked.

"Computer programming," Jake said.

"Like you did for Jamal's dad?" asked Frank.

"Kind of the same," Jake said. "I can't really say too much about it, but I did some of the programming to help run the new security system. They're not going to single me out or anything. The press conference is mostly to announce the first phase of the system coming online."

Frank and Joe nodded. Frank spotted 2510 Smith Street and pulled into the parking lot. "Here you go," he said. "Home sweet home."

"Home sweet hovel is more like it," Jake said. Joe helped him out the side door of the van, and Jake wobbled a bit as his legs hit the pavement.

"Don't worry," Jake said. "I can make it."

"If you don't mind, we'll walk you to your door—just to be sure," Joe said.

Jake nodded. "Okay. I guess that's all right."

"After all," Frank added, smiling, "we wouldn't want to have to tell Vanessa and Jamal that you fell down while in our care."

Jake smiled back weakly. "No. I guess you wouldn't."

18

As Jake fumbled in his pockets for his keys, Joe spotted someone familiar. "Hey, Frank," he said, indicating a guy in a black leather jacket walking on the far side of the parking lot. "Isn't that Jay Stone, Vince Morelli's pal?"

Frank nodded. "I wonder what he's doing here?"

"Stoney?" Jake said. "Don't worry about him. He lives in the apartment across from mine. Keeps to himself mostly."

"When he's not out making trouble with Morelli," Joe said.

Stone walked out of sight as Jake finally fished out his keys. The three teens walked toward the building.

"Do you know what kind of car Stone drives?" Joe asked.

"No idea," Jake said. "Why?"

"Just wondering," Joe said.

On their way to the door, they passed a large oak tree. Posted on one side of it was a Take Back Our Streets poster. It featured a smiling picture of Councilwoman Hamilton and the slogan "Securitech Supports Safe Students and Citizens—Campus rally and press conference, 10:30 A.M. tomorrow."

"Those popped up all over campus today," Jake said. "I think they want a big turn-out for the cameras."

"Understandable," Joe said.

Jake put his key in the lock and opened the door to the building. "I'm on the second floor," he said.

He pulled out another key and checked his mailbox but found nothing inside. He shut the box then walked up a stairway to the right of the door. Joe and Frank followed. At the top of the stairs, they came into a darkened hall.

"I can't believe it," Jake said. "The lights are out again." The only illumination in the hall was from a dim red emergency exit sign above their heads and from another at the far end of the hall.

"Does this happen often?" Joe asked.

"Occasionally," Jake said. "I'll call the super and he'll have it fixed by morning. Don't worry, my room's not far, just three doors down on the left."

"Hey, listen!" Frank hissed.

They all stopped and peered into the darkness.

Someone else was in the hallway with them, and as their eyes adjusted to the darkness, they could see that that person was fumbling with Jake's door.

3 Online On Campus

Frank pulled out his keychain and turned on the attached penlight. He shone the faint beam toward the intruder at the same time that Joe yelled, "Hey! What are you doing there?"

The figure at the edge of the flashlight's beam jumped, and all three teens heard something land softly on the carpeted floor. Joe and Frank rushed forward with Jake following just behind.

The figure looked as if she might take off. She stopped, though, when she saw Jake. "Jake," she said, much relieved, "you scared me!"

Jake let out a long sigh as well. "It's okay, guys," he said. "It's only Cindy. You gave us quite a scare, too. Cindy, these are the Hardy brothers, Frank and Joe."

"Hi," Cindy said, still looking a bit nervous. She

21

was a short, thin girl with bleached blond hair cropped very short. She wore tattered jeans and a white T-shirt.

"Nice to meet you," Frank said. Joe nodded his agreement.

Cindy squatted down, scooped something off the floor, and slipped it into her purse. Frank and Joe couldn't make out what it was. "Some stuff spilled out of my purse when you startled me," Cindy explained.

"What were you doing?" Joe asked.

"I tried the door, but there was no answer," Cindy said.

"Cindy's my girlfriend," Jake said, then corrected himself. "*Ex*-girlfriend. But we're still friends."

"She still hasn't told us why she's here," Frank said.

"I'm sorry," Cindy said a bit defensively. "Can't a friend just drop by to say hi? Besides, I don't know what business it is of yours."

"Well, Jake's had kind of a rough evening," Frank explained. "We're just looking out for him."

For the first time in the dim light, Cindy noticed the handkerchief tied around Jake's head.

"Oh!" she gasped. "What happened? Are you all right?"

"I got hit by some stray bottles," Jake said. "It's nothing."

"Jake could really use some rest," Joe said.

"Well, I wasn't going to stay," Cindy said. "I just came to say, hi, like I said. I wanted to remind Jake about the paper we have due tomorrow."

"Are you in Professor Firestein's class, too?" Frank asked.

Cindy nodded. "Yeah."

"What do you think of the course?" Joe asked.

"It's okay," Cindy said. "I've had better classes."

"Thanks for dropping by," Jake said to Cindy. "I remembered the paper. I'm going to work on it right now, and I'll drop it off tomorrow morning before the press conference."

"Are you still going to that thing?" Cindy asked.

"I have to," Jake said, a bit exasperated. "It's part of my job."

"I won't keep you then," Cindy said. She turned and walked down the hall in the opposite direction.

Jake put his key in the lock and opened the door. "Thanks for the lift," he told the Hardys.

"No problem," Frank said. "You sure you're okay?"

"Yeah," Jake said, gently touching his head. "I'll be fine, thanks. Just have to get to work."

Joe and Frank nodded. "Maybe we'll see you tomorrow, then," Joe said.

"Maybe," Jake said. "I'd invite you in, but I've got a lot to do."

"We understand," said Frank.

23

"Maybe I could buy you a soda some other time," Jake offered.

"Sure thing," Joe said.

"Well, okay. Great. See ya. Bye," Jake said. He went inside his apartment and shut the door.

Frank and Joe headed for the exit. When they got out the front door, Joe said, "I don't know about you, but he didn't look fine to me."

Frank nodded. "He looked worn out even before he was hit. Do you think it's just overwork?"

"Could be," Joe said. "We probably should have taken him to the hospital, had that cut checked out."

"What were we going to do, drag him to the emergency room against his will?"

"I don't know, but I wish we'd done more," Joe said. "I think Jamal's right—something's going on with Jake."

"We'll just keep an eye on him like Jamal suggested," Frank said.

"Good thing we've got a few days off from school." Frank nodded.

As they walked to the car, they passed the oak tree again. The poster for the next day's rally had been torn and a mustache drawn on Councilwoman Hamilton's face.

"Vandals?" Joe suggested.

"Either that or anarchists," Frank said with a

smile. "Or maybe someone who doesn't like the councilwoman."

"I'm not sure I like her either," Joe said. "This whole security camera business makes me uneasy."

"I know what you mean," Frank agreed. "It seems like an invasion of privacy."

When they reached the van, Joe hopped into the driver's side. Frank rode shotgun as they headed for home.

Jamal knocked on the Hardys' door just as they were finishing a late breakfast. Laura Hardy, Joe and Frank's mother, answered the door and showed Jamal into the kitchen.

"You guys going to this Securitech press conference thing?" Jamal asked.

Frank took a gulp of milk and said, "I think so. And you?"

"Yeah. I promised Vanessa I would. By the way, what did you guys think about Jake?"

"Something's definitely going on with him," Joe said, then put a forkful of scrambled eggs into his mouth. "We're just not sure what, yet. Might just be overwork."

Jamal nodded. "Maybe. I'm still worried, though."

"We'll keep an eye on him," Frank said. "How did you and Vanessa hit it off?"

"Great!" Jamal said, grinning. "We've got a lot in common: sports, music, movies. I promised to take her up in one of Dad's planes sometime."

Joe took his dishes to the sink, rinsed them off, and put them in the dishwasher. Frank did the same.

"Glad to hear it," Joe said. "Are you meeting her at the rally?"

"Afterward," Jamal said. "She's going to be onstage for the press conference. A lot of Securitech employees are."

"Want to ride with us?" Frank asked.

"No thanks," Jamal said. "Vanessa and I might want to do something afterward."

"You old smooth mover," Joe said, smiling.

The three friends headed out, and fifteen minutes later Joe pulled the van into a Bayport Institute of Technology parking lot near where the rally was being held. Joe gave a low whistle. "Look at all the news vans," he said to Frank.

"Looks like more cameras than at the march last night," Frank said. They spotted Jamal parking his car on the other side of the lot and jogged over to meet him.

"Quite a party," Jamal said as he got out of his sedan. "Look at the size of this crowd. Mostly students, I'd guess."

"They're probably curious, just like us," Frank said.

"Let's see if we can get good seats," Joe replied.

They started walking across the campus lawn to where a podium and grandstand had been set up. They passed a small group of orderly protesters carrying signs reading, Security, Not Securitech, and Cameras Don't Equal Security, and other similar messages.

"Obviously a teen threat," Joe said sarcastically as they passed the group.

"I don't know about these folks," Jamal said, "but did you see the Kings around?"

"You mean Vince Morelli and his bunch?" Frank said. "No. Did you?"

"I saw a couple of them hanging near the edge of the crowd. Morelli, Stone, Bettis, and some girl I didn't know," Jamal said.

"Bettis used to be on the football team with me," Joe said.

"Until he dropped out of school," Frank added. "What were they doing?"

"Just hanging out," Jamal said. "Hey, there they are now."

Morelli, Stone, and Bettis were making their way through the crowd, moving parallel to the Hardys, toward the platform. Howard "Harley" Bettis was a beefy teen, about an inch shorter than Joe. Morelli

27

and Stone looked hostile, as usual. All three were wearing their black leather jackets with *Kings* painted in red and yellow on the backs.

"Look at them," Jamal said. "You'd think they were a gang."

"They are," Joe said. "Well, gang wannabes, more like it. Morelli has a room above his old man's garage. They hang out there fooling around with computer equipment."

"The police have suspected them of several petty crimes," Frank said, "but they've never been able to pin anything on them."

"What do they do for a living, if they're not in school?" Jamal asked.

"Stone is in school," Joe said, "but the others just hang out, taking odd jobs—"

"Possibly illegal jobs," Frank put in.

"Sometimes they do some car repair work in the garage, I know," Joe said. "I'm not sure who'd take a car there, though. It's not a nice part of town. There's a girl in my class who hangs out with them, too, Missy Gates. Maybe she's the girl you saw."

"Could be, but she's not with them now," Jamal noted. "Come on. There's a spot over by that tree with a clear view of the stage."

Jamal led Frank and Joe to a spot under a big maple tree that was just turning red, and they all set-

28

tled in to wait for the press conference. The three of them scanned the podium but didn't see their friends. "I don't see Jake or Vanessa," Jamal said.

"Maybe they're not here yet," Frank suggested.

"Could be," Joe agreed. "Hang on . . . Councilwoman Hamilton's moving toward the podium."

Hamilton was a tall, thin woman with short-cropped reddish brown hair. She was immaculately dressed in a maroon business suit and wore a round gold pin on her lapel. She tapped the mike to make sure it was working.

A smattering of applause greeted her along with one loud boo from close to the Hardys' left. The brothers spotted Morelli and his Kings friends just a short distance away.

"Welcome," the councilwoman said, ignoring the Kings. "It's good to see so many fine young people joining us today. The Take Back Our Streets campaign is mostly for you, you know. Young people have the right to walk the streets of Bayport in safety."

"What about safety from police harassment?" Stone yelled.

"You know, I never thought I'd find myself agreeing with Jay Stone," Joe whispered to Frank. "But after yesterday outside the coffee shop . . ."

Frank and Jamal nodded in reply.

"Safety for everyone is the responsibility of each

29

one of us," Hamilton continued. "Though some selfish people would have us think otherwise." She smiled at the crowd and Stone sneered back at her. Hamilton took no notice. "Since our mayor is out of town on important business, it is my pleasure to introduce a prime mover in making Bayport a safer place to live—Clark Kubrick of Securitech Industries."

A strong burst of applause rang from the crowd, broken only by catcalls from the Kings and the dim sounds of a protest chant from the placard carriers near the back. Hamilton stepped aside and let the man behind her step to the microphone. Kubrick was a tall, well-dressed man in his middle thirties. He had long black hair, tied back, and wore a tie with a pattern of cartoon characters on it.

"Kubrick seems pretty popular with the college set," Joe whispered.

"He should be—he employs enough of them," Jamal whispered back.

"Thank you. Thank you so much," Kubrick said, acknowledging the applause.

"Down with Big Brother!" Stone shouted.

"What do you know," Frank whispered. "Stone must have read a book once."

"Maybe he just saw the video," Joe countered.

"Well, thank most of you anyway," Kubrick said

with a slight chuckle. The crowd laughed. Kubrick showed the cartoon on his tie to the crowd. "Despite my tie," he said, "I'm here to talk about a very serious matter today—the future security of Bayport. A future, I'm happy to say, that many of you have had a hand in bringing about."

The crowd applauded. Frank noticed that Morelli and his crew were clowning around, making faces and mugging for one another. Not more than a half-dozen people separated the Hardys and the Kings.

"As you know," Kubrick continued, "many of Securitech's most valued employees are BIT students. Without them, we couldn't activate this new security system today. For the first phase of this program, we've put Securitech cameras in the most crime-ridden areas of the city. It is our hope that the system will reduce youth crime and violence by half in the first year. While the areas we activate today are limited, by the end of next year we hope to cover all of Bayport in a high-tech security blanket."

"Cover *yourself* in a blanket!" Vince Morelli shouted. His companions made rude noises. Some of the crowd chuckled nervously.

Joe looked at Frank. "Should we quiet those guys down?" he asked. "They're making it seem as though all teenagers are idiots."

"They're the only ones who look like idiots," Frank

whispered back. Nevertheless, he saw Joe edging closer to the Kings. Frank was well aware of his brother's hot-headed nature and kept close to Joe. Jamal followed, too.

"Now," said Kubrick, "I'd like to introduce you to some of the fine students who worked with us on this project. They're one of the main reasons we decided to hold this rally and press conference at BIT Without them, we wouldn't be where we are today."

Councilwoman Hamilton stepped to the mike beside Kubrick. "These exceptional young people, some of them still in their teens, are to be commended for not slipping into laziness and hooliganism." She looked at both the orderly protesters and the Kings, now just a dozen feet from the Hardys, as she spoke.

Kubrick glanced at Hamilton as though her impromptu remark had caught him off guard. He recovered and said, "If our student employees would step onto the platform, please."

A small crowd of students did so. Kubrick began introducing those who had worked on the project.

As the list of names reeled on, Frank said, "I don't see Jake."

"There's Vanessa, though," Joe added. Then, mischief in his voice, he turned to Jamal and said, "Wave hi to your new girlfriend, Hawkins."

Jamal nudged Joe with his shoulder good-naturedly. "She's not my girlfriend, Hardy."

Joe bumped him back. "Not *yet* anyway," he said, smiling.

"A lot you know about romance, Hardy," Jamal countered. "Your idea of a date is anything you don't have to pay for."

Frank rolled his eyes. Joe assumed a boxer's stance.

"Well," Joe said to Jamal, "your idea of a date is taking a girl to a high-school boxing match." He threw a few shadow punches in Jamal's direction.

"Not any match you're in, Hardy," Jamal said. "I like a fight to last more than one round." He dodged and wove and threw a few shadow punches back.

Joe was about to counter when suddenly he felt Frank's hand on his shoulder. He turned and realized that much of the crowd was staring straight at him.

"And that," Hamilton's voice boomed over the P.A. system, "is exactly the kind of hooliganism that I plan to prevent!"

4 Wrongly Condemned

"Hey," Joe called out, "we were just fooling around." But his explanation was drowned out by Hamilton's voice on the P.A.

"It's bad enough that they have to waste the valuable time of our speakers with their rude remarks, but now they flaunt their violent ways in our very midst," Hamilton said, her voice icy cold.

"That wasn't us shouting," Jamal protested, "that was . . ." But when he looked to where the Kings had stood a minute ago, they were gone.

"Some people," Hamilton continued, "seem to feel that their rights supersede those of everyone else. They seem to think that they have the right to fight and steal and disrupt an event that other people are enjoying."

The Hardys and Jamal could feel the heat of the

34

crowd's stare now. They looked around for someone to bolster their story, but if anyone knew they weren't the culprits, no one stepped forward.

"Look," Frank said calmly, "I think you've got us confused with somebody else."

"I don't think so, young man," Hamilton said. "I know exactly who you are. You're the type of person that our Securitech system is designed to protect us against! In another few minutes, we'll activate the system and your kind will be banished from Bayport forever!" She stepped back from the microphone in triumph and the crowd applauded.

Joe saw a chance for them to slip into the crowd and motioned to Frank. Jamal followed and the three of them slunk away. "I think we should be safe near the parking lot," Joe said. Behind them, they could hear Kubrick talking again.

Jamal shook his head. "Man, I've never been so humiliated in my life. I hope Vanessa didn't see that. I'll never live it down."

"We caught a bad break," Frank said, "but we should have been more careful. Did either of you see Jake in that crowd?" Joe and Jamal both shook their heads.

"I don't get it," Jamal said. "He knew he was supposed to be here."

"Maybe we should blow off this rally and head

35

over to his place," Joe said. "It's only a few blocks away."

Before they could leave, though, a familiar figure ducked out of the crowd in front of them.

"Nice going," Cindy said. "I didn't think you guys had it in you. Good job sticking it to the authority figures."

Frank shook his head. "That's not what we were doing," he said.

"Sure looked like it to me," Cindy said.

"It was a case of mistaken identity," Joe insisted.

"Do I know you?" Jamal asked.

"I don't think so," Cindy replied.

"She used to be Jake's girlfriend," Joe said.

Jamal nodded. "That must be it. I'm Jamal, a friend of Jake's. Pleased to meet you." He extended his right hand.

She shook it. "Cindy," she said.

"Have you seen Jake around?" Joe asked. "We were looking for him."

Cindy shook her head. "Nope. Haven't seen him all day. Anyway, I thought you guys were way cool up there. Keep up the good work." Before any of them could respond, Cindy slipped back into the crowd and disappeared.

"Funny," Jamal said, "she doesn't really seem like Jake's type."

"Well, they're in a computer class together, so maybe . . ." Joe said, letting his voice trail off.

"Let's make doubly sure Jake's not here before we go to his place," Frank said.

They found an unobtrusive spot near the back of the crowd, well away from the protesters. Kubrick finished introducing his BIT employees and got back into the meat of his speech.

"This system," he said, "is state of the art digital technology. Our cameras now cover downtown, outside the mall, and this campus, as well as several other 'danger areas' around town. Phase One of the Securitech project will cut down on muggings, vandalism, pickpockets, and other types of crime."

An assistant rolled out a podiumlike platform from one side of the stage. Atop it sat an oversize green button. "When we press this ceremonial button," Kubrick said, "the Securitech system will come online and all of us in Bayport will be much safer than we were the moment before."

He and Hamilton exchanged smiles, then they stepped forward and pressed the button together. The crowd applauded wildly.

"We can all sleep safely knowing Securitech is on guard," Hamilton said, beaming. She took Kubrick's hand and held it up like a champion prize fighter's.

Kubrick leaned forward. "We wish you all a very

good—and safe—day," he said, calling the press conference to an end. Members of the media surged forward to take pictures and get interviews. The student employees of Securitech shambled off the stage and into the thinning crowd.

"I still don't see Jake," Frank said.

"Neither do I," Joe said.

"Let's ask Vanessa about him," Jamal suggested. "If he was here, she should know where to find him."

Joe looked toward the stage where reporters were still milling about. Councilwoman Hamilton was eating up the publicity as she smilingly shook hands and granted interviews. Kubrick was doing the same. Joe spotted Vanessa in a group of students not far from the stage.

"Talking to her is a good idea," Joe said, "if we can avoid Hamilton and company while doing it."

Frank nodded agreement. "No sense getting our faces on the front page if we can help it."

"I don't feel much like giving interviews, either," Jamal added. "We're lucky the reporters didn't snag us in the middle of the rally."

"Yeah," Joe said. "I hear reporters like talking to us tough-guy criminals."

"Let's just look for an opening and get to Vanessa if we can," Frank suggested.

They didn't have to wait long. Kubrick and Hamilton soon led the reporters away from the stage and toward a hall that had been set up as a reception and interview area. As the reporters left, the Hardys and Jamal walked toward the stage.

Vanessa met them halfway, frowning. "What were you guys doing?" she asked, her voice a mixture of anger and puzzlement. "I didn't think you were the type to disrupt an event that way."

"Honestly," Frank said, "it was a case of mistaken identity. We weren't the ones yelling at the stage. We were just in the wrong place at the wrong time."

"Joe and I were just horsing around," Jamal said. "Might not have been the best time for it, I admit, but . . ."

"Anyway," Joe said, finishing his friend's thought, "we weren't really fighting, and we didn't mean to cause a ruckus."

Vanessa crossed her arms over her chest and said, "Well . . ."

"To tell you the truth," Frank said, "not to excuse my barbarian brother and our friend here, I think Councilwoman Hamilton was looking for something to punch up her speech. I don't think she's very tolerant of people our age."

Vanessa smiled slightly and nodded. "I kind of got that idea from her speech. I've heard her daughter is a bit of a troublemaker, too. So that would make sense."

"Just too bad we fell into her trap," Joe said.

"Sorry if we embarrassed you, Vanessa," Jamal said.

"That's okay," Vanessa said, her smile widening. "Nobody knows that you guys are friends of mine."

"If we want to keep it that way, we should move away a bit," Frank said half seriously.

"Let's go over by the science building," Vanessa said, pointing to a nearby structure. "It's pretty much press-free over there."

"We were looking for Jake during the speeches," Frank said as they walked, "but we didn't see him. Was he onstage with you?"

Vanessa shook her head. "Nope. He didn't show. I'm not sure that Kubrick noticed, with everything else going on, but Jake's absence is sure to show up on Jake's time card. I'm a bit worried about him."

"We were thinking about checking his apartment," Joe said, "to see if he's there."

Before Vanessa could respond, though, someone called to her from the science building.

"Robinson! Hey, Robinson!"

The voice came from a chubby, middle-aged man with glasses and a goatee. The gray business suit that he wore didn't seem to fit quite right. He had been standing in the doorway to the science building but started jogging toward the teens when they stopped walking after hearing his call.

"Who's that?" Joe whispered.

"Professor Firestein," Vanessa said, a touch of hostility in her voice.

Before anyone could ask her what was wrong, though, the professor had caught up to them.

"Robinson," he said, "are you still friends with Jake Martins?"

Vanessa crossed her arms over her chest and said, "Yes . . . ?"

"Well," Firestein said, "I've been trying to reach him all day. He's not answering his e-mail or phone. I've left messages on his answering machine, but he hasn't returned my calls."

"Maybe he's out," Vanessa said defiantly.

"Well, if I don't hear from him soon, he'll be out for good. I'm tired of his excuses, and I won't give him special treatment any longer."

Firestein pushed his glasses up on his nose and continued. "You tell your friend that if he doesn't have his paper on my desk in the next hour, he'll be out of my class—just like you."

5 Harsh Realities

"That's a little harsh, isn't it?" Frank said.

"I'm a teacher, not a nursemaid," Firestein said. "I've cut Martins enough slack as it is. If you're friends of his, you'll give him the message. I'm not going to waste any more of my valuable time trying to get in touch with him. I thought he showed promise as a computer programmer, but maybe I made a mistake." He looked at Vanessa as he said this, implying perhaps that she had been a mistake as well.

Vanessa looked as if she might snap back at the professor, but before she could, Jamal stepped forward. "We'll deliver your message, professor," he said.

"See that you do," Firestein said. He turned and stalked back into the science building.

When he had gone Vanessa said, "Sometimes I just want to punch that guy."

"Probably wouldn't be good for your college career if you did," Frank said.

Vanessa sighed. "Honestly. Sometimes I think that college is overrated."

"What did he mean about Jake being out of the class like you?" Joe asked.

"I dropped out of Firestein's class earlier in the year," Vanessa said.

"Work load too much?" Jamal asked.

"Something like that," Vanessa said. "I've been making a lot of money at Securitech, and his class was interfering with that. I couldn't do both, so . . ." She shrugged her shoulders. "Plus, I just don't like the man."

"It's a required course, isn't it?" Frank asked. "That's what Jake told us."

"It is," she said, "but I'm hoping someone else will be teaching it next year. I'll take it again before I get my degree—if I don't quit and go full-time at Securitech."

"You'd leave school for the job?" Jamal said.

"I'd rather not, but if I have to, yes. Business is booming in high-tech right now, and sometimes a year on the job is worth more to a potential employer than a year in college."

43

"That works so long as high-tech is booming," Frank said, "but if it busts . . ."

Vanessa laughed. "With more people going online every year, I don't see that happening. Computers are the place to be. If Jake was smart, he'd drop Firestein's class, too, and increase his workload at Securitech."

"I've read that people with degrees in computer science make more money in the long run," Joe said.

"That may be true," Vanessa replied, "but I haven't given up on my degree yet, despite Professor Firestein. Until I get that degree, though, I want to earn as much as I can, and if I have to drop a class or two to do it . . ." She smiled and shrugged again.

"Well, I want to make sure that Jake can make that choice for himself," Frank said. "We need to find him and find him fast, before Firestein kicks him out of class."

Joe and the others nodded.

"Right," Jamal said. "Vanessa, do you know some other places to look for Jake besides his apartment?"

"We could call work, for a start," she said. "Though since he missed the rally, I doubt he's at the office. There are a few other spots around campus we could check out, too."

"Great," Frank said. "You two check the campus, Joe and I will look at his apartment and then Java John's. Jamal, do you have your cell phone?"

"In my car," Jamal said.

"Good. We can keep in touch, then," Frank said. "Call if you find him. We'll do the same."

"Let's get to it," Joe said. He began to jog back toward the parking lot. Vanessa and Jamal headed toward where Jamal had parked.

As they got to the parking lot, they saw a large crowd of people and reporters standing around a pink sedan. Councilwoman Hamilton stood in the middle of the group, anger blazing on her face. Through the crowd the Hardys could see that the sedan's tires had been slashed.

Hamilton pointed at some nearby students carrying protest signs. "They did this," she said loudly enough so everyone could hear. "They slashed my tires before the system went online just to humiliate me!"

The students looked sheepish. The reporters pointed their cameras at the protesters. A cop on the scene began to take notes.

"Let's get out of here before she decides to blame it on us," Joe whispered. Frank nodded and they quickly moved toward their van.

When they got there, Frank climbed behind the wheel and Joe picked up the cell phone. Joe dialed Jake's number while Frank drove.

"No answer," Joe said. Then added, "Who do you think really slashed Hamilton's tires?"

"Who knows?" Frank said. "It could have been the Kings—they did cut out pretty early. On the other hand, the councilwoman strikes me as the kind of person who makes enemies pretty easily."

"I haven't known her long and I'm a fan already," Joe said.

Frank laughed, then abruptly stopped and said, "Check that out." He pointed at a small box atop a light pole at the edge of the parking lot.

Joe looked up and saw a Securitech camera busily scanning the area. "I expect we'll be seeing a lot more of those in the future," he said.

It took them only a few minutes to drive to Jake's apartment. As they went, both brothers noticed numerous rally signs posted along the way. Nearly all of them had been defaced.

"I wonder if they got any of that on camera," Joe said.

"Maybe not," Frank replied. "I haven't seen any Securitech gizmos since we left the campus."

"But Jake's is just a few blocks away," Joe said.

"A few blocks, and a million miles in terms of political influence," Frank noted.

They pulled into the lot and got out of the van. When they entered Jake's building, they ran into Jay Stone coming downstairs. He was wearing his Kings jacket and combing his hair.

46

"Hey, Hardy boys," Stone said mockingly. "Solved any big crimes lately?"

"A few, Stoney," Joe said, "but we haven't connected you to any of them—yet."

Stone pushed past them and out the door. "Well, good luck," he called back. "Don't take any red herrings."

"You know," Joe said when Stone had gone, "you might be right, Frank. He *did* read a book once."

"Probably just an abridged version," Frank said. "Let's check on Jake."

The two of them went upstairs and knocked on Jake's door. When no one answered, Joe tried the knob. "It's unlocked," he said, and pushed the door open. The brothers stepped inside.

The room was dark and smelled vaguely of unwashed dishes. Curtains had been drawn over the windows, so the only light came from a computer screen on the far side of the room. Papers lay strewn all over the floor. A body lay slumped on a couch facing the door.

The body moved as Joe found a light switch and flicked it on.

"Jake!" Frank cried.

Jake opened his eyes and stared blearily at the brothers. He was still wearing the same clothes he had been in the day before, and Frank's handkerchief was still wrapped around his head.

47

"We were worried about you, man," Joe said.

"What time is it?" Jake asked.

"Nearly twelve-thirty," Joe replied.

Jake sat bolt upright on the couch, instantly awake. Then he put his hands to his temples. "Ow! My head! What a killer headache. I have to get to that rally."

"Rally's over," Frank said. "We ran into Professor Firestein afterward. He said you need to get your paper to him before one, or you're out of the class."

"Oh, man," Jake said. "I've really messed up now!" He dashed into the bathroom and came out with two aspirin and a glass of water. "Thanks for waking me up, guys," he said. "You saved my life."

"I doubt that," Joe said. "But maybe you should still have a doctor check out your head. That headache could be a sign of a concussion."

"Don't have time for that now," Jake said, gathering up a pile of papers from the floor. He stuffed the papers in a small briefcase and headed for the door. "Besides," he said, "it's just overwork. I'm sure of it."

The Hardys looked at each other skeptically. "Look, why don't you meet us at the mall after you drop off your paper," Joe said. "We can have lunch and talk it over."

"Sounds great," Jake said, not looking at them as he headed out the door. "How about at that potato place, Spud Spa. It's in the food court."

48

"Okay," Frank said, "see you there in an hour or so."

"Thanks, guys," Jake called over his shoulder as he raced down the hall. "Lock the door when you leave."

Joe looked around the room. Apparently, the mess was by design. "Who'd want to steal anything?" Joe asked.

Frank shrugged. "A lot of students can't keep their lives together—never mind their rooms."

"Shall we poke around a bit before we go?" Joe asked. "See if we can find out what's bugging him?"

"I don't think we've come to that yet," Frank said. "It's not like we're investigating a crime—just checking on a friend for another friend."

"Well," Joe said, "at least we found him. Let's call Jamal and head for the food court. I'm famished."

Frank used the cell phone to get in touch with Jamal as they drove to the mall. Jamal and Vanessa were relieved to hear that the Hardys had found Jake and that Jake was on his way to Firestein to deliver his paper. They agreed to meet the Hardys at the mall in fifteen minutes.

As Frank and Joe drove to the mall, they couldn't help but take note of the Securitech cameras along the way.

"I notice that there weren't many cameras in the poorer parts of town, like near Jake's," Joe said. "But there's plenty of security out here."

Frank nodded and frowned. "Kubrick said they were protecting the places that most needed it. I guess he thinks poorer folk don't get robbed."

"I'm not sure whether to hope that they get cameras in the poorer areas, or just hope this whole project goes away," Joe said.

"I know what you mean," Frank replied. "This business of being on camera all the time gives me the creeps."

They got to the mall a few minutes later and, because the lot was crowded, parked near the back. "Never hurts to do a bit of walking," Joe said as he pulled the van into an empty spot.

As they walked toward an entrance, Howard "Harley" Bettis cruised past them on his motorcycle. He revved his engine as he went by, causing both Hardys to jump. Harley laughed and zipped away.

"Those Kings," Joe said.

"Hey, there's Jamal and Vanessa," Frank said. They were waiting for them outside the mall's main entrance. Frank and Joe jogged to where their friends were standing.

"Glad you found Jake," Jamal said. "How'd he look?"

"Not so hot," Frank said. "But we didn't have time to quiz him—he was in too much of a hurry."

50

"Well, at least he got Firestein off his back," Vanessa noted.

"He's supposed to meet us at the Spud Spa in half an hour," Joe said. "With a little luck . . . Hey!"

"What is it, Joe?" Frank asked.

Joe pointed. "See that SUV? I want to get a better look at it." He started to walk toward a red vehicle with tinted windows.

"Do you think that's the one that threw those bottles at Jake?" Jamal asked.

"Let's find out," Frank said, following his brother.

As they approached the car, though, the SUV suddenly backed out of its space and took off.

"They've seen us," Joe cried. "Let's get 'em!"

6 Who's Chasing Whom?

"I'll try to cut them off," Frank said. He darted between two cars and headed for the end of the next row.

"Good idea," Joe called. "I'll get the van." He sprinted across the lot toward where they had parked.

"What should *we* do?" Jamal shouted after the brothers.

"Wait here!" Joe shouted back. "When Jake shows up, tell him we'll be right back!"

Frank, sprinting between the cars, smiled at his brother's confidence. Frank didn't feel quite so cocky. While the arrangement of the lot favored him, the SUV was a lot faster than he was. He knew he would be lucky to catch the car on foot.

Fortunately, he was tall enough to see over the roofs of the cars as he darted through the aisles; the

SUV was a big target as well. Frank chose a path that would put him between the vehicle and the nearest exit.

He glanced back and saw Joe hop into their van and start the engine. The odds were tilting in their favor. The SUV was moving quickly, as if its driver wanted to get out of the mall in a hurry. Fortunately for the Hardys, other cars and one-way aisles made it difficult to speed through the parking lot.

Frank's plan worked. He found himself at the end of an aisle just as the SUV turned into it. There was no one between him and the SUV. He waved his arms, trying to get the car to stop. He couldn't see the driver through the tinted windows.

The SUV came straight at him. It didn't slow down.

At the last possible moment, the car turned right, darting through an empty space between a sports car and a van and into the next aisle. That aisle ran in the opposite direction, but the SUV's driver didn't seem to care. The car zipped to the end of the row, turned right, and darted off toward a nearby exit.

Frank kicked himself for not seeing the escape route. Now he'd lost the SUV.

A van screeched to a halt at the top of the aisle. Frank realized it was Joe. He sprinted to the van, threw the passenger side door open, and hopped in.

Joe took off, turning left at the exit, and then left again onto the wide road running beside the mall.

"Joe, are you sure that was the right SUV?" Frank asked as he buckled himself in.

"Why else would they be running from us?" Joe asked. "Besides, check out the bumper sticker."

Frank read it. "Chaos Rules. The same sticker you saw the other night!"

"Right," Joe said. "And the license plate's still covered with mud. Any questions?"

"Just one," Frank said. "Who's driving that car?"

"We'll find out soon enough," Joe said, pushing the gas pedal down.

The SUV crested a hill, and they lost sight of it temporarily. When the van bounced over the hilltop, the Hardys were just in time to see the SUV turn off onto a smaller side road.

"Whoever's driving that car has pretty good reflexes," Joe said. He slowed the van enough to make the turn, then gunned it again.

"We're just lucky that these roads are pretty deserted," Frank replied.

"I don't know," Joe said. "I'd be pretty happy for a traffic jam right about now. That way we'd be able to catch up to them on foot."

"Doubting your driving skills, Joe? Maybe I should take the wheel," Frank kidded.

"No way, bro. That'd be like switching quarter-backs once you'd made it into the playoffs."

The van turned left, taking the brothers even far-ther into the semirural countryside surrounding the mall. The SUV bounced over the hilly road with the Hardys' van still pursuing.

"You know," Frank said, "I was just thinking: one of Morelli's gang used to drive a red SUV before he dropped out of high school. I don't remember who it was, though."

"Well, we just saw Bettis driving his Harley, so we know it isn't him. It might be Morelli or Stone, though."

"I don't think it's Stone," Frank said. "He lives in the same apartment building as Jake. If it was his car, we'd probably have spotted it in the apartment parking lot."

"That leaves Morelli," Joe said, "if it's one of them at all."

"It could be Missy Gates as well," Frank said. "I don't think we can rule her out just because she's a girl."

"She doesn't seem to be the bottle-throwing type," Joe said, "though I don't know her very well."

"If she's in with the Kings, she's probably got it in her," Frank said. "They also could have members that we don't know about."

"Whoever is behind the wheel is a pretty good

driver," Joe said. They topped another hill, and a long stretch of deserted road lay before them. Because of Joe's expert driving, the SUV was only four car lengths away now. "Let's see how many horses they've got under the hood," Joe said with a twinkle in his eye.

He floored the accelerator and the van leaped forward. The SUV's driver saw them coming and swerved toward the center of the road, trying to cut them off.

Joe swerved in the other direction, the van's tires catching the edge of the shoulder and kicking gravel and dust into the air. The SUV cut back in front of them so Joe couldn't pass on the right.

"Yow!" Frank said. "Whoever they are, they don't want to get caught, that's for sure."

Suddenly the SUV cut left, barreling across the road and heading straight for the trees that lined the left side of the road. For a moment the Hardys thought the car would crash.

The SUV's driver obviously knew the road better than Joe did. The vehicle darted between the trees and onto an unpaved road running into the forest.

"Rats!" Joe blurted. He hit the brakes and cut the wheel hard. The van's tires squealed, and it fishtailed as Joe brought it around in a 180-degree turn. The cell phone flew from its cradle on the dash, but Frank caught it before it could sail out the window.

"Good thing we didn't have any hot coffee in here," Frank said.

They'd missed the turn, but Joe backtracked and swung the van onto the dirt road. They barreled down the dirt road, dust from the car ahead of them obscuring their view.

"Watch out for wild animals," Frank said. "I'd hate to hit a deer at this speed."

"They'll hit it first," Joe said grimly.

Suddenly they topped a hill and saw the end of the woods ahead of them. The SUV skidded out of the dirt road and toward a paved stretch.

"What road do you think that is?" Joe asked.

"Barmet Boulevard, I'd guess," Frank said. "We've cut through the woods toward a pretty high-class suburb."

"Let's hope we catch them before they hit one of those subdivisions. We'll never find them in all those winding roads."

The Hardys' luck held. The SUV was only a short distance ahead when they exited the woods. In fact, the driver seemed to be having trouble controlling the vehicle. The red car swerved from side to side.

"They've blown a tire!" Frank said as the car swerved off the road and into a ditch by the shoulder. The SUV came to a sudden halt.

Joe pulled up on the shoulder and skidded the van

to a stop just a short distance from the stranded car. The SUV's passenger-side door opened, and a woman got out.

"Are you crazy?" she screamed. She was about the Hardys' age, of medium height and build, and had scraggly brown hair. She was wearing a Kings jacket.

"Missy Gates," Joe said. "So you're the one who threw that bag of bottles at Jake. We suspected you Kings might be behind this."

"You are in a world of trouble, Joe Hardy," Missy said. "You and your snotty brother, too."

"Don't say anything, Missy," a voice called out from inside the van. "I've called the cops, and I've called my mother, too."

"Who's in there with you?" Joe asked. He still couldn't see through the SUV's tinted windows.

"It doesn't matter," Frank said. "We've got them and the cops can sort it out." The brothers could hear police sirens even now.

"That's what you think, wise guy," the voice said. The door to the driver's side opened and out stepped Cindy.

Frank and Joe looked at Jake's ex-girlfriend, then at each other. "This doesn't make any sense," Joe said.

"You bet it doesn't make any sense," Cindy said angrily, "you chasing us all over the place."

"We know you hit Jake last night," Joe said.

Cindy sneered. "Prove it." Missy Gates laughed.

With the wail of sirens, two police cruisers pulled up, one from either direction. They took up positions on either side of the Hardys' van. The officers inside the cars got out and walked toward the group.

"What's going on here?" the lead officer asked.

"I'll tell you what's going on," Cindy said. "These guys have been chasing us all around town, and they nearly got us killed!"

7 The Eye of the Beholder

"That's not true," Joe protested. "They hit a friend of ours with some bottles, and we were trying to catch up with them."

"He's lying," Cindy said angrily. "These two are troublemakers. They've been following us, harassing us. Check the video tapes of this morning's rally at BIT. They were making trouble there, too."

Joe's face reddened. "We have witnesses . . ." he began.

Cindy tugged at Missy's arm. "So do I," she said.

"That's right," Missy said. "These guys were chasing us. We were afraid for our lives."

Frank stepped forward. "I'm Frank Hardy, and this is my brother, Joe," he said. "Officer Con Riley or Chief Collig will vouch for us."

"Well," Cindy said, "I'm Cindy Hamilton, and my mother—the *councilwoman*—will vouch for me."

Joe and Frank looked at each other, more than a little surprised at Cindy's revelation.

The officer who had been talking to the group scratched his head. "I think we had all better go downtown to straighten this out," he said. "Hop into the cruisers. I'll have one officer stay with the stranded car, another will bring the van."

"Sounds good," Frank said. He and Joe headed toward the squad car indicated by the cop.

"Just make sure my mother knows where you've taken me," Cindy said. She and Missy got into the other squad car.

As the Hardys got into the back of the cruiser, Joe turned to Frank and said, "Well, this case just took a turn for the worse."

Forty-five minutes later the brothers found themselves sitting in an interview room at the Bayport PD. Across the table from them sat Con Riley, their main contact on the police force.

"I think I can get the chief to go easy on you," Con said. "Your father's with him now, but you guys really stepped over the line this time. Whatever possessed you to chase them like that?"

"They threw bottles at a friend of ours last night and hit him on the head," Joe said. "What were we supposed to do, just let them get away?"

"You and your friend should have reported the attack when it happened. Now it's just your word against Cindy's—and her mother's a councilwoman."

"We had no idea her mother was Councilwoman Hamilton," Frank said. "We didn't even know who was in the car until it blew a tire and stopped."

"The point is," Con said, "that you shouldn't have been chasing them in the first place. You should have reported this to the police rather than zooming around the countryside like NASCAR drivers."

Joe bristled. "But their license plate was covered with mud, just like it was last night. We couldn't report them—we didn't know who they were."

"But you should have reported the incident, nonetheless," Con said sternly. "We don't have a police or even a hospital record that an attack happened. We have nothing."

Frank frowned. He knew Con was right. They should have insisted that Jake go to a hospital to report the incident.

"What about covering the license plate with mud," Frank said. "That's pretty suspicious, isn't it?"

62

"The girls say that happened when you chased them down that dirt road."

"We weren't chasing them," Joe said, stubbornly folding his arms across his chest. "We were trying to apprehend them."

"For a crime you didn't report?" Con said. "I expect better of you boys."

Frank put a hand on Joe's shoulder. "We expect better of ourselves, too."

Con leaned back. "Look," he said, "I know you boys, and I'm inclined to believe your explanation of events. But Chief Collig isn't so generous—you know how he feels about amateurs. Plus, he's got the tape evidence against you."

"What tape evidence?" Joe and Frank asked simultaneously.

"The Securitech tapes of the beginning and end of the chase," Con said.

"Then you can see them tearing around the mall parking lot like madwomen."

Con shook his head. "I'm afraid not. There are no cameras in the mall lot. What the tape shows is you chasing them down the highway outside the mall. We lost you for a while, and then picked up the chase again when both cars skidded onto Barmet Boulevard. The tapes look pretty bad for you."

63

Both brothers slumped in their chairs. "Then the tapes are lying," Joe said.

"Or at least," Frank added, "they don't show the whole truth."

Con sighed. "Try convincing the chief of that."

The three of them sat in silence for a few minutes. Then the door opened and Fenton Hardy stepped in. Frank and Joe's father looked grim. "I think I've got things squared with Chief Collig," he said. "He's willing to release you into my custody."

"What about Cindy and her friend?" Joe asked.

"I think they're being released, too," Mr. Hardy said. "But I wouldn't worry about them right now. You boys are in enough trouble on your own."

Joe and Frank nodded. "That tape doesn't show the whole story, Dad," Frank said.

"Be that as it may," Mr. Hardy said, "we should get out of here before the chief changes his mind and decides to charge you with endangerment or reckless driving. Let's go."

Both Hardys stood and followed their dad to the door. As he put his hand on the knob, Fenton Hardy turned back to Con Riley. "Thanks for keeping things under control, Con," he said.

"Yeah, thanks," Frank added.

Con nodded. "Just keep your noses clean," he said. "Hamilton knows how to play hard ball."

"So do we," Joe said under his breath, but if anyone heard, he didn't respond.

As the Hardys walked to the front door of the station, a commotion at the front desk caught their attention.

"I can't believe you're letting them go." Councilwoman Hamilton's voice rose above the hustle and bustle of the station house. "They disrupt our press conference this morning, the chase my daughter this afternoon! What does someone have to do in this town before they're arrested?!"

Joe seemed about to say something, but Fenton Hardy put a hand on his son's shoulder and steered him and Frank toward the door. "You can't win a PR battle with her," Mr. Hardy whispered.

"I wouldn't be surprised if they're at the bottom of the recent wave of vandalism, too," Hamilton added. Cindy and Missy were standing beside her, looking smug. Cindy stuck her tongue out at Frank as the Hardys went out the door.

As they exited, they saw a gang of reporters' vans pull up to the curb. At a nod from Fenton, the three of them headed away from the descending mob. "Things are going to be pretty hot for you two the next couple of days," Mr. Hardy said.

"We can handle it, Dad," Frank answered.

"We didn't do what they said," Joe added. "Those tapes don't show the whole story."

"I believe you," Fenton said. "I'm going to look into the legalities of this taping business a bit further. I haven't been comfortable with it, but now . . ." He let his voice trail off. "In any case," he continued, "you boys need to lay low for a while."

"We will, Dad," Frank said.

"Good," Mr. Hardy said. "Your mother and I will see what we can do, but we can't solve this problem for you. You've made a powerful enemy in Councilwoman Hamilton. Try to stay out of her way."

Both Hardys nodded. "We will," they said.

"Good," Mr. Hardy said. "I got your van out of impound. It's up the street. Probably you should just head home."

"We will," Frank said, "but we left some friends hanging at the mall. We need to check in with them first."

"Don't worry," Joe said. "We'll keep our noses clean."

"See that you do," Mr. Hardy said. He left the boys at the van and walked down the street to his car.

"Well," Joe said as he and Frank got into the van, "this has been one of the worst days of my life."

Frank slipped behind the wheel and said, "The day's not over yet."

When they got to the mall they found Jamal sitting on a bench outside the main entrance. "I was wondering what happened to you guys," he said, just a tinge of exasperation in his voice.

"Sorry about that," Frank said, "we kind of got carried away."

"By the police," Joe added.

Jamal's eyebrows arched. "What happened?"

"It's a long story," Joe said. "We'll fill you in later. Where are Vanessa and Jake?"

"Jake never showed," Jamal said. "We tried to get him on the phone, but there was no answer. After a while we decided that Vanessa would go and look for him while I waited here for you."

"You loaned her your car?" Joe said in mock horror. "Pretty bold move, Hawkins."

Jamal chuckled and shook his head.

"Can we call her on your cell phone?" Frank asked.

Jamal shook his head and took the phone out of his pocket. "Nope. I kept the phone in case you tried to call."

"Guess we should have," Frank said. "Where was Vanessa going to check first?"

"Work, I guess. Then a couple of places Jake hangs

out. Maybe he had trouble getting a cab out here or something."

"He could have taken a bus," Joe said.

"I know," Jamal replied. "But you know how Jake's been acting lately. Vanessa said he'd forget his head if it wasn't attached. I'm supposed to meet her back at my house later."

"Well, why don't we check Jake's apartment," Frank said. "We can call on the way there."

"Wouldn't he answer the phone?" Jamal said.

"Maybe he unplugged it," Joe said. "And he did get a pretty nasty knock on the head the other night."

Jamal nodded agreement and the three of them piled into the Hardys' van. Twenty minutes later they pulled up outside Jake's apartment. Jamal spotted his car in the lot.

"Hey, Vanessa must be here," he said.

"Maybe she's found Jake," Joe said.

"Let's hope," Frank said. The three of them got out of the car and made their way upstairs to Jake's apartment. When they got to the door, they found Vanessa turning the knob, though they couldn't tell if she was going out or in.

"Find him?" Jamal asked.

His voice startled Vanessa, and she jumped before recovering her wits. "Not yet," she said. "He wasn't at work or any of his usual hangouts. I just got here."

Frank stepped forward. "Is the door unlocked?" he asked. Vanessa nodded. "Let's check it out," Frank said.

He opened the door, and all four of them went in. Joe turned on the lights as they entered.

Jake was collapsed on the floor in the middle of a pile of papers.

Vanessa gasped. "He's not breathing!"

8 Urgent Mystery

Joe and Frank rushed forward and knelt to check on Jake. Frank lifted one wrist to check his pulse, and Joe bent forward to look for other signs of life.

After a few moments Joe said, "He's alive, but his breathing is very shallow."

Frank turned to Jamal and said, "Call nine-one-one."

Jamal found the phone and dialed.

"What do you think happened?" Vanessa asked.

"We can't be sure, yet," Frank said. "Someone could have attacked him, but maybe he's just exhausted."

"He didn't look very well when we saw him earlier today," Joe put in.

"The ambulance is on the way," Jamal said, hanging up the phone.

"Is there anything else we should do?" Vanessa asked.

"I don't think so," Joe said. "Jake doesn't seem to be in any distress. It would probably be a mistake to move him. We'd better just wait and let the paramedics do their job."

It didn't take long for the ambulance to arrive. Joe rode in the ambulance with Jake. Jamal took Vanessa and Frank in his car. Frank figured he'd come back for the van later. The hospital wasn't far from campus.

The Hardys and their friends had to stay in the waiting room while the doctors examined Jake. Half an hour later a young doctor came out to talk with them.

"Your friend's going to be okay," the doctor said. His name tag read Dr. Sean Kendall. "Looks like he got a pretty nasty bump on the head sometime recently."

"Last night," Joe said. "He was hit by some bottles."

"He probably should have come in sooner," Dr. Kendall said. "He's pretty dehydrated, too, and seems to be suffering from exhaustion."

"How soon can he go home?" Vanessa asked.

"He could probably go home right now, but I wouldn't recommend it," Dr. Kendall said. "We'd like to keep him overnight for observation."

"That sounds like a good idea," Frank said.

"Does he have any relatives in the area?" the doctor asked.

"No," Vanessa replied. "They all live out of state. Why?"

"Just a precaution," Dr. Kendall said. "We got his school insurance information, so he's covered, but it's always nice to have a contact who knows his medical history. We'll try to track his folks down through the insurance company."

He scanned the Hardys and their friends. "You folks should probably get some rest, too. You look pretty worn out yourselves. Exams?"

"Some school stuff, yeah," Joe said.

"Come on," Frank said. "We can check in on Jake tomorrow morning." He and the others turned and headed for the door.

When they got outside, it was already dark. Jamal said, "Do you guys want a lift back to your van?"

Frank shook his head. "It's not that far, and we could use the exercise."

"Okay," Jamal said. "I'll take Vanessa to her dorm. We can check back with each other tomorrow."

"Good idea," Joe said.

Vanessa and Jamal headed for Jamal's car, and the Hardys began to walk back to Jake's apartment.

"We're not that starved for exercise, you know," Joe said.

"I know," Frank replied, "but I figured a walk might clear our heads."

"This case sure is a puzzler," Joe said. "We still don't know what's going on with Jake, but things seem to be getting more complicated by the minute. I mean, who would have guessed that Cindy was the councilwoman's daughter?"

"And who'd have guessed that she threw those bottles at Jake?" Frank said. "The question is, why did she do it? A girlfriend/boyfriend thing maybe?"

"They did break up," Joe said, "but that's about all we know. And she might not have been the one who threw the bottle. Maybe Cindy wasn't even in the car last night."

Frank nodded. "You mean, she might have lent the car to Missy?"

"Or somebody else. Or the Kings could have 'borrowed' the car without Cindy even knowing."

"I hadn't thought of that," Frank said. "But if that's so, why did Cindy flee when we tried to get close to her car at the mall today?"

"I don't know," Joe said. "Guilt seems the most likely explanation, but . . ."

"One thing's for sure," Frank said, "it won't get any easier to figure this out with Councilwoman Hamilton stirring things up."

Joe looked up, checking for cameras on the light poles as they walked. He didn't see any. "Politics," he said. "I'm not sure whether to wish for more of those cameras, or wish they'd just disappear."

"I don't think we can count on Securitech to get to the bottom of this, Joe. We'll probably have to do it ourselves."

Joe nodded. "As usual."

"Another thing's been bugging me," Frank said. "Who are the vandals? Is Cindy one of them? The Kings? Someone else? Exactly what acts of vandalism have been committed lately? And are the vandals carrying out a grudge against Councilwoman Hamilton, or Securitech, or are they just mad at the world?"

"You know, Frank, it would make sense if Cindy was involved. A lot of kids don't get along with their parents."

"Or their ex-boyfriends," Frank added. "Could be. Maybe she's the source of Jake's troubles. That would explain why he doesn't want to talk to anyone about it. I know I don't feel much like talking if Callie and I have a fight." Callie Shaw was Frank's girlfriend.

"Or me and Iola," Joe said, referring to his own girlfriend, Iola Morton. "But we know Jake's been having trouble at school, too. And missing that rally this morning couldn't have helped his status at work."

"So, one way or the other, Jake's in trouble. I don't know if we can sort it out for him."

Joe shook his head. "I don't know, either. We

74

should keep trying, though." He stopped and thought a moment. "You know," he finally said, "it would be pretty ironic if Cindy were part of the teen crime wave that her mother is trying to prevent."

"Yeah, it would," Frank said. "But as you said, a lot of kids don't get along with their folks."

"I'm glad our parents are so reasonable," Joe said.

Frank nodded. "Me, too. I was pretty sure Dad would bawl us out for the business with the cops, but he took it all pretty calmly."

"I think this Securitech business has him a bit worried," Joe said. "I'm just glad he's on our side."

They began walking again. Just before they came to the edge of campus nearest to the hospital, Harley Bettis and Vince Morelli cruised by on their motorcycles. The Kings sneered at the Hardys when they saw them.

"Let me wipe the smiles off their ugly faces," Joe said, but Frank held him back.

"No, Joe," he said. "Let's just head for home. We've had enough excitement for one day."

"Those guys are like cockroaches," Joe said, fuming. "They just keep popping up."

The brothers had to cross the BIT campus on their way to Jake's apartment. As they walked across the broad lawn, Joe noted the Securitech cameras. He pointed one out to Frank.

"Why don't I feel safer?" Joe asked. Frank chuckled.

At the edge of the campus, they spotted Professor Firestein dressed in a blue jogging suit. He wasn't jogging, though, just walking.

Frank nudged his brother. "Hey, let's make sure Jake dropped off his paper," he said. Joe and Frank walked toward Firestein. "Professor," Frank called.

Firestein looked in their direction. "Do you need something?" he asked, slightly perturbed. "My hours are posted on my office door."

"We're not students," Joe said. "We were just wondering if Jake Martins dropped his paper off. He wasn't feeling well and had to go to the hospital. We were hoping he delivered the paper before he got sick."

"I remember you now," Firestein said. "You're friends of his. I talked to you earlier in the day. Yes. I got the paper. He got it in on time—barely. Now, if you'll excuse me, I want to continue my regimen." He picked up his pace and jogged away from the Hardys. After he'd gone just a short distance, though, he slowed down again.

Joe and Frank followed him with their eyes.

"Don't ask if Jake is okay or anything," Joe said sarcastically.

"I can see he's not going to win any Teacher of the Year awards," Frank added. "Think he treats everyone that way, or just Jake's friends?"

"Judging from what Vanessa said, I'd say everyone.

Come on, Frank, let's get the van and head for home."

Ten minutes later they reached Jake's apartment building and reclaimed their van. As they climbed in, Jay Stone called down to them from his apartment window.

"Hey, Hardy boys—saw you on TV. Didn't you bring the media with you this time? Or are you waiting for another ambulance?"

The brothers ignored him and drove off.

Later that evening, after dinner, they were sitting in their own living room.

"What a lot of problems," Frank said. "Jake, Securitech, BIT, Hamilton, Cindy, the Kings . . . It's like a huge puzzle, but I have no idea how to begin putting the pieces together. Do you think we're trying to make a mystery where there isn't one, Joe?"

Joe yawned. "Could be," he said. "Maybe Jake is just burned out from work and school. That doesn't explain who the vandals are or who threw those bottles at him, or why. Could be Cindy, could have been Missy or one of the Kings, or even someone we haven't thought of yet. We just don't have enough information to figure it out."

Frank got up and stretched. "Maybe our brains will work better tomorrow. I'm heading for a good book and a good night's sleep."

Joe got off the couch and headed for his room, as well. "Me, too," he said. "Things will probably look better in the morning."

The brothers were woken next morning by their dad calling to them from the hall.

"Frank, Joe," Fenton Hardy said, "come out here a minute, will you?"

The Hardys walked sleepily into the hall.

"What's up, Dad?" Frank asked.

"Con's here to see you," he said.

"Con?" Frank said. "What's he doing here this time of the morning?"

"He's not paying a social call," Fenton Hardy said, his voice grim. "He wants you to answer a few questions."

9 Suspects List

"What does Con want, Dad?" Joe asked.

"He won't say," Mr. Hardy said. "Do you want me to call our lawyer?"

Frank and Joe shook their heads. "That's not necessary, thanks," Frank said.

"We haven't done anything," Joe added.

"Well, maybe I can sit in on the questioning then," Mr. Hardy said. "I'll go talk to Con while you get dressed. We'll wait for you downstairs."

A short while later Joe and Frank found their father and Con Riley seated in the study. Both held steaming cups of coffee. Glasses of orange juice for Joe and Frank were set on coasters atop Fenton Hardy's desk. The brothers each took one and then sat down.

"What's up, Con?" Joe asked.

"Boys," Con said, "we had some trouble last night, and we were wondering where you were when it happened."

"What kind of trouble?" Frank asked.

"A break-in at Councilwoman Hamilton's office," Con said. "Since you had some trouble with her and her daughter yesterday, we have to question you about it. Where were you around seven fifteen last night?"

Frank and Joe thought for a minute. "We were walking back to the BIT campus from the hospital," Joe said. "We had to take our friend Jake there. He was pretty sick."

"Do you have any witnesses?" Con asked.

"Professor Firestein saw us," Frank said. "But that would have been closer to seven-thirty. Jamal and Vanessa left us at the hospital just before seven, though. They know we didn't have our car with us."

"I hope that will be good enough to satisfy the councilwoman," Con said, rising from his chair.

"What do you mean?" Frank asked.

"Just that Councilwoman Hamilton has it in her head that you two were behind the break in."

"Her office is downtown, isn't it?" Fenton Hardy said. "There should be a Securitech tape showing exactly who broke in. It doesn't show Frank and Joe, does it?"

"Well . . ." Con said, hesitating. "There's a problem there."

"What kind of problem?" all three Hardys said together.

"The Securitech system was down in that area last night," Con said. "Just a temporary glitch in the programming, they say."

"But long enough for a crime to happen to the system's major supporter," Frank said.

Con nodded. "Pretty frustrating, really," he said.

"Quite a coincidence," Mr. Hardy said.

"Yeah," Joe agreed, crossing his arms over his chest.

"Was anything taken?" Frank asked.

Con straightened his uniform. "No. Nothing. The place was pretty badly trashed, though—papers scattered everywhere, furniture and computers smashed. A real mess."

"I'm betting her daughter did it," Joe said.

"What?" Con asked, puzzled.

"Joe's right," Frank said. "It could be Cindy Hamilton. All this would make sense if she's angry at her mother for some reason. Maybe she wasn't trying to hit Jake the other night. He was carrying one of her mom's flyers at the time. Maybe she was just lashing out at her mom."

"That would explain the slashed posters, too," Joe said. "Remember the first night we met her? When we went into Jake's apartment that night, the poster on that tree was okay. Then we met Cindy. When we came out again, the poster had been slashed."

"You boys don't have proof of any of this," Con said.

"Not yet," Frank said.

"But we will," Joe added.

"Now, boys," Con said, "you should keep your noses out of this. The police can handle it."

"The police want our necks in a noose," Joe said angrily. "So does Councilwoman Hamilton."

"Calm down, Joe," Fenton Hardy said. "There's nothing to be gained by getting all worked up." He winked at his sons. "I'm sure the police can handle the situation. Why don't you just sit tight for a while."

"Your dad's right, guys," Con said. "Relax. Take it easy. We can handle this. We don't have any direct evidence against you, and I'll make sure the council-woman doesn't railroad you into jail. Just relax and take it easy. Stay home. Hang with your friends. But keep your noses out of police business."

Frank and Joe glanced at their dad, who nodded.

"Yeah. Okay," Frank said.

Con went to the door. "All right, then. Don't bother getting up. I can find my way out. And, Fenton, thank your lovely wife for the coffee. It was ex-cellent."

"I will," Mr. Hardy said. After Con had left the

house, he turned to his sons. "I didn't want to say anything in front of Con, but this whole thing makes my blood boil. I know you two didn't do anything wrong, but this crazy security system makes it seem as though you did. I'm going to spend the day talking to people—see what kind of political angles I can pursue. I'm not sure how we let Big Brother sneak into our town, but I want to revoke his work visa."

Frank and Joe both smiled.

"While I do that," Mr. Hardy said, rising from his chair and heading for the door, "I want you to promise that you'll stay out of the way of Councilwoman Hamilton."

"If she'll stay out of our way," Joe said.

"Joe . . ." Mr. Hardy said, disapproval in his voice.

"Yeah, okay. Sorry, Dad," Joe said. "We'll lay low."

"We promise," Frank said.

"Good," Mr. Hardy said. "I'll see what I can do." He left the room.

Frank sipped his orange juice. "So, what do you want to do while we lay low?" he asked.

"We ought to check on Jake," Joe said. "Go to the hospital, see how he's doing."

"Good idea," Frank said. "We shouldn't run into the councilwoman while we're doing that."

But when they arrived at the hospital, they discovered that Jake wasn't there.

"What do you mean?" Frank asked the young woman behind the reception desk. The name on her tag read Julie Scott.

"He's not registered in any of our rooms," Ms. Scott said.

"Did something happen to him?" Frank asked. "Did he get transferred to another hospital?"

"I'm afraid I can't tell you that," she said. "Hospital regulations."

"But we brought him in last night!" Joe protested.

The young woman shrugged. "Sorry."

Joe looked ready to boil over with frustration. Fortunately, Frank spotted someone who might help them. "Come on, Joe," he said. "We wouldn't want Julie to get in trouble with her bosses. Sorry to bother you, Ms. Scott."

Frank pulled Joe past the reception area and into one of the corridors connecting the hospital to the clinic next door.

"What's up?" Joe asked.

"I just saw the doctor we talked to last night walking down this corridor," Frank said. "Maybe he'll be more responsive than the receptionist was."

They caught up with Dr. Kendall a minute later. He had a clipboard and was busy making notes on it.

"Long shift?" Frank said as the brothers skidded across the tile floor to where Dr. Kendall was standing.

He smiled at the brothers. "Nope. Last night was my weekly night in emergency. Today I'm doing the clinic and making my rounds. I do get to sleep sometimes."

"What happened to Jake, Dr. Kendall?" Joe asked. "The receptionist wouldn't tell us."

"The kid you brought in last night?" Dr. Kendall asked. "He checked himself out shortly after you left—against my advice, I must admit. College students are sometimes hard to reason with—or understand. No offense."

"None taken. Do you know where he went?" Frank asked.

"Home, I hope," the doctor said. "At least, that's what I told him to do."

"Thanks, doc," Joe said. "We'll go check on him right now." He and Frank headed for the door.

"Remind him to rest when you see him," the doctor called. "Otherwise, those headaches could come back. Concussions aren't anything to trifle with. And he should pick up that prescription I called in for him if he hasn't already."

"Will do," Frank said. "Thanks again, doc."

He and Joe hit the parking lot and hopped in their van. Ten minutes later they pulled up in front of Jake's apartment. They zipped up to the second floor and knocked on Jake's door. When they got no answer, Joe tried the knob.

"Locked," he said.

Frank frowned. "Hmm. Where to next?"

"Well, it's Saturday, so he shouldn't be in class. We could check his work or maybe the library or some restaurants. Why don't we call Jamal and Vanessa, see if they know."

"Good idea," Joe said. The brothers went back to their van and got the cell phone. Frank called Jamal first and got Vanessa's number from him. Unfortunately, neither one had seen Jake.

"Vanessa said she had to stop at work today to pick something up," Frank said. "She promised to see if Jake had checked in. She thought he was working today."

Joe, sitting behind the wheel, said, "Where does that leave us, then?"

"I'm not sure," Frank said. "I did find out one thing, though: Jamal dropped Vanessa off before the break-in occurred last night."

"You're not thinking she's a suspect," Joe said.

"I think it's too early to rule anyone out," Frank said. "We know that *we* didn't trash that place. And I think it's funny that Hamilton's office got broken into just when the Securitech system was out in that part of town. The only people we know who might have had access to information about the system being down are Jake and Vanessa."

"And Jake checked himself out of the hospital before it happened."

"Yeah," Frank said. "I don't know what motive either one of them would have for trashing the office, though."

"I still think Cindy's our main suspect," Joe said. "We know that she—or one of her friends—was involved with that bottle throwing. She's in Jake's computer class, and she used to go out with him. That might give her access to Securitech somehow."

"It might," Frank said. "For now, though, the only people we know with Securitech access are Jake and Vanessa."

Joe nodded. "It would be a real bummer if Vanessa had anything to do with this," he said. "I think Jamal really likes her."

"Yeah," Frank said. "We can't rule out the Kings, either. They've got some computer skills—although probably not enough to tackle something like Securitech. I don't know. . . ." He looked thoughtful for a moment. "I still think you're right. Cindy's our best suspect, but—"

Bang! Something hit the side of the van. Both brothers jumped. When they looked out the window, they saw Cindy Hamilton standing next to them with her fist clenched. She must have sneaked up and banged on the side of the van with her fist as the brothers talked.

"Speak of the devil," Joe said.

"What are you two doing in there?" Cindy asked. "Plotting some new crime?"

"Plotting to put you behind bars is more like it," Joe said.

She smiled. "You're not up to it, blondie. You make any moves toward me and my mom'll have you in jail so fast that it'll make your head spin."

"I'm sure she thinks you're a little angel," Joe said. "But we know better, don't we?"

"I don't know what you *think* you know," Cindy said.

"What are you doing here, Cindy?" Frank asked.

"Hey, it's a free country, isn't it? I can walk where I want."

"If you're coming to visit Jake," Joe said, "he's not home."

"Who said anything about Jake," Cindy replied. "I'm just out for a walk." She waggled her fingers at them. "Stay out of trouble, boys." Then she walked away, heading in the direction of the BIT campus.

"She's some piece of work," Joe said, watching her go.

Frank nodded. "You know," he said, "she could have come here to visit Jay Stone. Maybe she's in deeper with the Kings than we thought."

"That would make sense," Joe said. "I wonder what the Kings are up to, though."

"Maybe just causing chaos," Frank said. "That's enough for some people."

"Hey!" Joe said. "There's Jay Stone now."

Sure enough, Stone was coming out of the apartment building. As he did so, though, he ducked to one side and pressed his back against the wall.

"What's he up to?" Joe asked.

A moment later they saw. Out of the building walked Jake. He looked worn out and unaware. As he moved forward a couple of steps, Stone stuck out his foot and tripped him.

10 Jake's Secret

Before the Hardys could yell a warning, Jake toppled to the ground.

The Hardys bolted from their van and raced toward Jake. Joe balled his hands into fists.

"Get away from him, Stone!" Joe shouted.

Stone backed away, his hands in the air as if to say "no problem." He chuckled. "No law against having a laugh at the expense of a nerd," Stone said.

"There's a law against assault," Frank replied.

"Hey," Stone said, "he should have looked where he was going."

"You might have a little 'accident' yourself," Joe said menacingly.

"Maybe later," Stone said. "Right now I've got errands to run. You Hardy boys should start your own scout troop," he said as he walked away.

Frank helped Jake to his feet. "You all right, Jake?" he asked.

Jake nodded and brushed off his pants. "I didn't see him," he said. "I must have fallen asleep. I thought I heard someone knock on my door, but by the time I got up, no one was there."

"That was us," Frank said. "We came to see if you were all right."

"My head still hurts," Jake said. "So I thought I'd go to the pharmacy to fill that prescription the doc gave me."

"You want to do that now?" Joe asked. "We could give you a lift."

"Maybe later," he said. "Right now, I think I'd better lie down again."

"No problem," Joe said. Jake turned to go back into the apartment, but as he did, his knees buckled. Frank and Joe lunged forward to support him under each arm.

"Thanks, guys," Jake said weakly.

They helped him upstairs and into his apartment. Jake walked to the couch and sat down. He leaned his head back so it rested on the back of the sofa and sighed.

"Is anything bothering you, Jake?" Frank asked. "You've seemed pretty strung out."

"Oh, man," Jake said. "I think I've done something really bad. I've been caught in the middle, and I just don't know what to do."

"Why don't you tell us about it," Frank said.

Jake let his head slump forward. "Yeah, okay," he said. "I guess I really need to talk to someone. At least a bit. You guys promise you won't tell anybody?"

"Who would we tell?" Joe asked.

"I don't know," Jake said. "The school, my boss at Securitech? I don't think the police would be interested, but . . ."

"We promise," Frank said.

Jake leaned forward and put his elbows on his knees. "I need this job at Securitech. I don't want to lose it. The pay is good, and it's giving me valuable experience. Plus, it'll look good on my résumé.

"But I want to stay in school, too. I want to get my degree in four years, not five or six. Maybe this class doesn't matter as much to Vanessa—working at Securitech seems more important to her."

"Are you talking about Professor Firestein's class?" Joe asked.

"Yeah. It's a good class, but very"—he paused, searching for the right word—"demanding. It's not just the demands on my time—though that's rough as well. I haven't had a lot of time for sleep lately."

He sighed before continuing. "When I started working at Securitech, I had to sign a confidentiality agreement—a piece of paper saying that I wouldn't reveal certain aspects of the work I do for them: computer codes, algorithms, and such. At the time I didn't think that would be a problem."

"But it's become a problem?" Frank asked.

"Well, one of Professor Firestein's recent assignments gave me the same kind of programming problem I've had to figure out at work. The only way to solve it is the same way I solved it for Securitech. So, to complete the assignment, I had to duplicate the code I'd used at work. But I think that may have violated my agreement with Securitech."

"And now you're afraid they'll fire you if they find out?" Joe asked.

"Yeah. I didn't have any choice, though," Jake said. "It was either that or flunk Firestein's class."

"Why didn't you talk to either your professor or your boss?" Frank asked.

Jake sighed again. "I remembered a couple of months ago when Vanessa tried to talk to them. Her workload had gotten too heavy for her to handle. She talked to both Firestein and Kubrick, but neither one had been sympathetic. Kubrick told her she'd have to make a choice between work and school; Firestein said the same thing. Vanessa chose to keep her job and dump the class.

"I didn't want to make that choice. The job gives me both money and good experience. And, as I said, the course is required to get into other classes that I need to be able to graduate on time.

"So I used some of the same code I'd used at Securitech. But it's been bugging me. I haven't had a good night's sleep since I got the assignment."

"Is that the paper you turned into Firestein yesterday?" Frank asked.

"That's the one," Jake said. "I don't even know why Firestein assigned that kind of program to the class. It wasn't on the syllabus we got at the beginning of the semester."

"What kind of program was it?" Joe asked.

"It involved security and control for remote sensing devices."

"Like the cameras at Securitech," Frank said.

"Yes, like the Securitech system. I wish I'd never gotten that stupid assignment. What else could I do, though? I didn't want to flunk the class. But if Kubrick finds out . . ." Jake didn't finish the thought.

Frank and Joe nodded, indicating they understood.

"You guys aren't involved in this," Jake said. "Do you have any ideas about what I should do?"

94

"Short of turning yourself in to Kubrick?" Joe said. "I understand that you don't want to lose your job, but—"

"I could be *sued* for violating that agreement," Jake said, almost frantic.

"That makes it trickier," Frank said.

Jake put his head in his hands and ran his fingers through his hair. He looked as though he was about to say something, but a knock on the door stopped him.

Frank got up and opened it. Vanessa stood on the other side. "Frank," she said, sounding surprised. "What are you doing here?" She looked past him and saw Jake sitting on the couch. Frank stepped back and Vanessa rushed into the room.

"Jake!" she said, obviously relieved. "There you are. I've been looking for you. Where have you been?"

"Um . . . sleeping mostly," Jake said.

"This place is a mess," she observed. "When was the last time you checked your e-mail or your phone messages?" Spotting the answering machine, she went over to it. The light on the machine was flashing. "Do you want me to play this message back?"

"You might as well," Jake said.

Vanessa pressed the playback button and made sure the volume was turned up. The machine beeped while the tape rewound. Then the clear, deep voice of Clark Kubrick, head of Securitech, came out of the speaker.

"Jake," the voice said, "this is Clark Kubrick. I've been trying to reach you for two days. Today is Saturday. I need to see you in my office at work today, or Monday you may not have a job."

11 Vanessa's Secret

"Oh, man!" Jake said. "I need to get in to work."

"I could drive you," Vanessa said. "I have to pick up something at the office. But we'd need to stop by my dorm first. I walked over here to check on you."

"We could drive both of you," Joe said.

"I hate to impose . . ." Jake began.

"No trouble," Frank said. "There's plenty of room in the van."

"Well, I'll take you up on the offer, too," Vanessa said, smiling.

"Okay," Jake said. "Just let me get a couple of things." He went into the bathroom, changed clothes, and cleaned up a bit. When he came out, he still looked haggard, but at least he was presentable.

Fifteen minutes later they pulled up in front of Securitech's downtown office. It was in one of the modern buildings on Bayport's waterfront. Jake hopped out of the van.

"We'll wait for you," Frank said.

"Aren't you going in, Vanessa?" Joe asked.

She shook her head. "I figure I'll stay out of shrapnel range. After Jake's through, I'll go in and pick up what I need."

"We'll park, then," Frank said. He chose a spot with a view of the Securitech door.

"I notice they've got good coverage of their office," Joe said, pointing at several cameras perched atop nearby light poles.

Vanessa smiled. "It wouldn't do to have foxes raid the henhouse," she said. "Bad for business."

"How do you like your job at Securitech, Vanessa?" Frank asked.

"It's great," she said. "The money is good, and the experience is very valuable."

"Worth quitting Firestein's class over?" Joe asked.

"Definitely worth it," she said.

"You said before that it was the class workload that made you quit," Frank said.

"Well . . ." she said, "I'm sorry if that's the impression I gave you. I just didn't feel like dragging the whole thing out right then."

"What whole thing?" Joe asked.

"The whole thing that I was caught in between Securitech and Firestein," she said.

"Oh?" Frank said. "What happened?"

"Well, when you work with a company like Securitech, you sign a nondisclosure agreement. That means you can't tell anyone about some aspects of your work—usually the programming," Vanessa said.

"Jake mentioned that," Joe replied.

"Right. He had to sign one, too. Everybody does. Anyway, earlier in the year, Professor Firestein gave us an assignment that came pretty close, I thought, to the part of the Securitech code I was working on.

"Like most things in Firestein's class, it was a do-it-or-hit-the-road assignment. I didn't want to get in trouble at either work or school, so I tried to talk it out."

"So, you talked to Firestein and Kubrick?" Frank asked.

"Right," Vanessa said. "And they were both pretty bull-headed about it. In one sense, I understand that Kubrick has a business to run and Firestein has a class to teach. Neither one was willing to help me out much, Firestein less, even, than Kubrick."

"So you quit the class," Joe said.

Vanessa shrugged. "As I said before, I needed the money more than I needed the class. And Kubrick's a nicer guy to be around than Firestein."

"Yeah," Joe said, "we got a taste of Firestein ourselves. Ran into him last night after dropping Jake off at the hospital. He didn't even seem to care that Jake was sick."

"That doesn't surprise me," Vanessa said. "He doesn't care much about anything but his computers and his programs and his research. I'd guess that Firestein's class is part of what's making Jake sick."

"I think you could safely say that," Frank said. He and Joe exchanged a meaningful glance. Vanessa didn't notice. Instead she leaned back in her seat behind the brothers.

"You know," she said, closing her eyes. "I'm really glad I got out of that class."

At that moment Jake came back out of the Securitech building. He looked even more pale than when he'd gone in. He climbed into the van and put his head in his hands.

"How'd it go, Jake?" Joe asked.

"Not so good," Jake said.

"Tell you what," Frank said. "It's about lunchtime. We'll treat you at Java John's, and you can tell us what happened. You're invited, too, Vanessa."

"Thanks, guys, but I still have a couple of things to check on here," she said. "You three go ahead. I'll catch a cab or something later." She got out of the van and closed the door behind her. "Good luck!" she called back as she walked up to the front door of Securitech. She inserted her passcard and went inside.

Frank drove to the coffee shop, a couple of blocks away. Since it was Saturday, they had trouble finding parking and had to walk a ways.

"We could almost have left the van at Securitech and walked from there," Joe said.

"Trouble with parking is it's hard to tell when you'll have trouble finding any," Frank said. "Right, Jake?"

Jake muttered a reply and the three of them went into Java John's. After they'd settled in and ordered, Joe said, "So what happened, Jake?"

"I got suspended from the company," he said, rubbing his hands through his hair.

"Suspended?" Joe said. "Why?"

Jake sighed. "The company got an anonymous tip that I'd divulged secret information—broken my confidentiality agreement. Kubrick suspended me indefinitely while the company looks into the accusation."

"Wow. That's tough," Frank said.

"I'd probably feel worse if I didn't deserve it," Jake said.

"Who do you think could have told them?" Joe asked.

"I don't know. I didn't really tell anyone what was going on—not until I talked to you guys earlier today. But Kubrick called my place before then."

"Could Vanessa have told him?" Frank wondered. "She said she was having a problem similar to yours, that's why she dropped out of Firestein's class. Maybe she figured out what was happening with you and turned you in."

"That's why she dropped out?" Jake asked. "I thought it was because of the workload." He shook his head. "I can't believe she would tell Kubrick. She's no rat."

Joe snapped his fingers. "Maybe it was Cindy," he said. "Jake, did you tell Cindy anything about your problem? She's in Professor Firestein's class with you, and she's been making a lot of trouble lately."

"We think she might even have thrown the bottles at you," Joe added.

Jake looked at the brothers with surprise and disbelief. "Cindy? I can't believe that either. Sure we broke up but . . . Besides, I never told her about the nondisclosure conflict."

"Could she have figured it out?" Frank asked.

"I don't see how," Jake said. "She's not very good in the class. I think she started going out with me to get help with Firestein's homework. Man, does my head hurt!" He rubbed his temples.

Joe and Frank didn't ask any more questions until the food came. Then the three of them sat and ate quietly. Jake seemed listless and took a long time to finish his sandwich. Even the coffee didn't seem to perk him up.

Finally Joe said, "Jake, we'll stay on top of this and try to figure out what's going on. Right now, though, I think we should take you home."

Frank nodded. "We should stop at the pharmacy and pick up that prescription for you on the way."

"No," Jake said, standing. "I can't impose on you guys any longer. You've been driving me around like a limo service. I can get home on my own."

"Well," Joe said, "if you won't let us drive you, at least take a cab. You're in no shape to walk."

"Yeah, okay," Jake said, nodding. "I'll take a cab."

Frank said, "I'll pay the bill. Joe, you get the cab company on the phone."

"Check," Joe said. He and Jake headed for the phone near the door. Five minutes later the three of them stood outside the café, waiting for the cab.

"You guys don't have to wait with me," Jake said. "I can do this on my own."

"We know that, Jake," Frank said, "but we'll feel better if we see you off."

"The cab company said they were a bit jammed up anyway," Joe added. "You might as well have some company while you wait."

The three of them made small talk until the cab

arrived. Frank and Joe waved goodbye to Jake and then headed for their van.

"You know," Joe said, "in the time we were waiting, we could have driven him to the pharmacy and then home."

"Yeah, I know," Frank said, "but you can't blame the guy for wanting to be independent."

The brothers rounded the corner. Their van was parked two blocks farther down the street.

When they were a block away, they caught sight of someone squatting by the van. The person was wearing a Kings jacket and appeared to be tampering with one of the van's tires.

12 Wolf in Kings' Clothing

"Hey, you! Stop!" Joe yelled.

The figure messing with the tire didn't turn. He just jumped up and took off running down the block toward the waterfront.

"Don't let him get away!" Frank said.

Both he and Joe took off after the vandal. Frank had done some running on the track team in school; Joe, too, was in top physical condition. Still, the person they were chasing now had almost a two-block lead on them.

"He's heading for the park along the waterfront," Frank said.

"If we lose him down there, we may never spot him among the trees," Joe added.

He and Frank redoubled their efforts. Slowly they

closed the gap between them and their quarry. They were only a block behind when the vandal entered the park.

The vandal was dressed all in black, aside from the red and yellow painted Kings jacket. Clouds had moved in, darkening the sky, which made it hard to see him as he darted through the trees.

"Looks like he knows this park," Joe said as he and Frank ran.

"Good thing we do, too," Frank said. "You keep following. I'll cut through the woods to see if I can head him off by the footbridge."

The brothers split up and went in opposite directions. Joe poured on more speed and was soon gaining on the runner, although the shadows made the fugitive harder to see.

In the distance Joe could make out the footbridge leading across an inlet of Barmet Bay. He couldn't be sure if the vandal was heading for the bridge or not, but he hoped Frank would be there. But before Joe reached the bridge, the fugitive suddenly ducked into the woods.

Joe sprinted after him. Brush slapped against Joe's body, and he had to duck to avoid low tree branches, but he managed to keep the guy in sight.

Suddenly they burst out of the woods and onto a path. Joe was barely ten feet behind the vandal now.

Putting all his strength into one lunge, he darted across the path and tackled the fugitive by the ankles.

The vandal went down hard, the air rushing out of his body in a great whoosh. Joe had taken a lot harder hits in his football career. Instantly he was up. He grabbed the fugitive's leather Kings jacket and turned him over, just as Frank dashed up behind him.

"I got to the bridge just in time to see you two dart into the woods," Frank said. "Good catch, Joe. Who is it?"

Frank and Joe stared in surprise at the person wearing the Kings jacket: Cindy Hamilton. Cindy spit out some dirt from her mouth and pushed her blond hair back from her dusty face. "Get off me, you brute," she sneered to Joe.

Joe backed off and let her get to her feet, but when she tried to run, he grabbed her by the arm. "Not so fast," he said. Cindy shook her arm to get free, but Joe didn't let go.

"You've got a lot to answer for, Cindy," Frank said. "The break-in at your mother's office, throwing bottles at Jake, trying to flatten our tire. I'm not sure why you're mad at the world, but it doesn't give you the right to hurt other people."

"A lot you know," Cindy said angrily. "When I tell my mother what you've done, the police will lock you two up forever."

"I think you're forgetting something," Frank said.

"What?" Cindy asked, contempt staining her voice.

"The last time you pulled one of your stunts, no one saw you but us. This time, though, you forgot something—the Securitech system. This whole area is blanketed by cameras. There's one near where we parked our van, and we passed a number of them in the park. This time the police will believe us, rather than you."

Cindy didn't say anything, she just smiled contemptuously.

"Come on," Joe said, pulling her by the arm. "We'll talk this over at police headquarters."

He and Frank marched Cindy back to their van. They checked the tires to make sure they were safe, then Frank drove while Joe sat in the back to keep an eye on Cindy.

"This is kidnapping, you know," Cindy said.

"Just think of it as a citizen's arrest," Joe said.

"What made you do it, Cindy?" Frank asked as he headed for the police station. "Your mother's a councilwoman, so your family must be doing okay."

"And your mother came rushing to your side after that car chase," Joe added. "You're even counting on her to get you out of trouble now. So how bad could your life be?"

"I'm not saying anything," Cindy said, folding her arms over her chest.

"My guess is that you just don't appreciate what you've got," Frank said. "I'm also thinking that you're probably still mad at Jake for breaking up with you."

"He didn't break up with me," Cindy said, sneering. "I broke up with him."

"What was it?" Joe asked, ignoring her disclaimer. "Was his work load too heavy? Did he choose school and Securitech over you?"

"And what about this Kings jacket?" Frank said. "Trying to shove some of the blame on your pals, or are you in deep with Morelli and his bunch? My guess is the first, because I doubt you have any real friends."

Cindy clenched her hands and fumed. Her face reddened. Finally she said, "Talk to my lawyer about it."

Joe and Frank chuckled. They figured their guesses had hit the mark. Cindy sat silently and steamed all the way to the stationhouse.

When they got there, the brothers escorted her into the building. Cindy went along grudgingly. As they approached the door, though, the Hardys noticed a small but wicked smile creeping across Cindy's face.

"Don't worry, Joe," Frank whispered to his brother. "We've got her on tape this time. The cops will have to believe us."

"Why do I feel she's got something else up her sleeve?" Joe whispered back.

Luck was with the Hardys. They ran into Con Riley just inside the stationhouse door.

"Joe, Frank," Con said. "What's up?"

"We caught her trying to flatten our tires, Con," Frank said.

"She did it right inside the Securitech blanket area this time," Joe added. "So there shouldn't be any question of guilt."

Cindy smiled. "These guys are liars. Call my mother. Get my lawyer. I want to prosecute them for illegal imprisonment."

Con looked from the Hardys to Cindy, and then back again.

"She's trying to weasel her way out of the rap," Joe said. "But we've got her dead to rights this time."

"Where did this alleged incident take place?" Con asked.

"On Scott Avenue," Joe said. "Down by the waterfront. She led us on a foot chase through the woods in the park."

"They chased me," Cindy said, "but only to harass me. I ran from them because I was scared."

Con showed them to some chairs near his desk. "Sit here while I try to figure this out," he ordered.

Con spoke briefly with a couple of other uniformed officers and then went to the phone and began making calls.

"When my mother finds out about this," Cindy said, "you guys are dead."

"What's she going to say when she finds out you're a petty criminal?" Frank asked.

In reply, Cindy just smiled.

After a few minutes, Con returned and beckoned for Frank and Joe to join him. Con took them aside so Cindy wouldn't hear them. "I've got some bad news for you, boys," he said. "I just had one of our men run the Securitech data from the areas you mentioned."

Frank and Joe looked at each other and smiled.

"Great, then, you—" Joe began.

Con cut him off. "I don't know how to tell you this," he said, "but it looks like there was some kind of problem in the system. That area has been blacked out for the last three-quarters of an hour."

"But—" Joe began.

"I know," Con said. "Rotten luck. You guys might want to get out of firing range before her mother gets here."

Frank quickly glanced at the door and said, "Too late."

Councilwoman Hamilton stormed into the squad room accompanied by a man Frank took to be a lawyer. Neither one of them looked very pleased. "Where's my daughter?" Hamilton said angrily. "What have you done to her?"

In response, Cindy jumped out of her chair and ran into her mother's arms. "It was those awful Hardy boys," Cindy cried. "They chased me in the park and brought me here against my will!"

"She was letting the air out of our tires!" Joe yelled angrily.

"Ha! He's lying," Cindy said. "They have no proof. They're just trying to make me look bad."

"I think we may have to let the courts settle this," Hamilton's associate said.

"Now, let's not be too hasty," Con Riley said. "Maybe we can work this out."

As Con tried to calm the Hardys and the Hamiltons, the police station suddenly grew busy. Another officer came up to Con and said, "Drop what you're doing, Riley. We need people downtown, pronto!" He whispered something more in Con's ear.

"Downtown?" Frank said. "What's going on?"

"Some kind of break-in," the officer said.

Con turned to the Hardys and the Hamiltons. "Folks," he said, "we're going to have to postpone this until another time."

"Another time . . . ?" sputtered Hamilton. "Why, that's outrageous." She stopped, though, as Cindy tugged on her sleeve.

"Come on, Mom," she said. "I don't think they'll

bother me again. Besides, I've got better places to be." She smiled maliciously at the Hardys.

"Well, if you think so, dear," Councilwoman Hamilton said. She turned to the Hardys. "Next time, though, I'll see you both in court."

Joe was about to say something, but Frank elbowed him in the ribs. Cindy, her mother, and her associate turned and left the police station.

Con Riley turned to the brothers as he pulled on his jacket. "Sorry about that, guys," he said. "But without any proof . . ."

"I don't understand why the cameras didn't catch Cindy," Joe said.

"Well, maybe this call explains it," Con said.

"What do you mean?" Frank asked.

"The break-in," Con said, "is at Securitech."

13 The Securitech Heist

"There was a break-in at Securitech?" Joe said. "How can that be?"

"I gather that the security system is pretty much automated on the weekend—and most other times as well," Con said. "That's the beauty of it. There are a few programmers who work on Saturdays, but no human systems operators."

"No human judgment, either," Frank said.

"And, apparently," Joe said, "no one watching the candy store."

"They didn't know there was any trouble until a technician came in to check the system," Con said. "I guess the main office got pretty messed up. I gotta run, boys." With that, he headed for the door.

"Mind if we tag along?" Frank asked.

"Fine by me," Con said. "Just stay out of the way."

A few minutes later Frank and Joe pulled up outside the Securitech offices. They didn't see Con, but Joe spotted Clark Kubrick standing outside. Yellow police tape was already stretched across the front of the building.

Joe and Frank walked up to the police tape so they could hear better. A police officer was standing next to Kubrick, taking notes.

"Nothing much taken!" Kubrick said angrily. "Maybe three computers doesn't seem like much to you, but one of those computers had our master control disc. It runs the whole system!"

"I'm sure you have a backup, Mr. Kubrick," the officer said. "Was that stolen as well?"

"Of course not," Kubrick said. "We keep our duplicates off site. That's not the point, though. A criminal with that disc might compromise our whole system!"

"Do you have any idea who might have pulled this job?" the officer asked.

"I think so," Kubrick said. "If I were you, I'd be looking for Jake Martins."

"Why is that, sir?" the officer asked.

115

"Because the trouble that caused the system to go down tonight was with the section of computer code that he wrote," Kubrick said. "Plus, I got a tip that he was compromising our security. I talked to him in my office earlier today about it. Plus, Jake had the expertise needed to shut off the camera systems selectively."

"Is that what happened here?" the officer asked.

"According to our preliminary analysis, that's why the cameras went down for about an hour earlier. That would have given Martins the time to break in, bust up the place, and take those computers."

"I'll have someone bring this Martins in for questioning," the officer said. She turned away from Kubrick for a moment and spoke into a walkie-talkie.

Frank nudged his brother. "Come on, Joe," he whispered. "We've got to talk to Jake." Joe nodded and the two of them headed for the van.

As Joe slid behind the wheel he said, "Man, this case just gets stranger all the time. I thought we had Cindy in the bag, but then the cameras go down. Not only do we not get her, but she couldn't have done the Securitech break-in because she was with us at the time." He pulled the van into traffic and headed for Jake's apartment.

116

Frank sighed. "The Kings could still be behind this somehow," he said. "Cindy has to be connected to them. Maybe she put them up to the job."

"I don't know, Frank," Joe said. "Call me crazy, but this break-in just seems to be out of Cindy's league—and out of the Kings', too. Sure, I can see them, or her, pulling off a petty crime or two. Some vandalism, shop-lifting, slashing tires, even throwing bottles. But this theft required both computer expertise and planning."

Frank ran a hand through his dark hair. "You're right. Cindy doesn't strike me as bright enough to pull all this off on her own. I don't think the Kings have that much brainpower, either. So who does that leave?"

"I hate to say it," Joe said, pulling the van onto Smith Street, "but Jake *is* a good suspect."

"Vanessa could be, too," Frank said. "We know she was at Securitech today. She could have set up the robbery. And she has the computer expertise."

"But what's the motive?" Joe asked. "That's what I'm having trouble wrapping my brain around. Money? I don't think Jake has time to spend any. And Vanessa seems to have enough money from her job. It would be foolish for either of them to jeopardize their careers by pulling a crime like this."

"I know," Frank said. "I have a feeling there's a piece missing from this puzzle."

"Me, too," Joe said. "Maybe Jake has some idea what that piece might be." He pulled the van into the parking lot next to Jake's building. As he did so, he saw that two police cruisers were parked outside.

As they watched, two police officers escorted Jake out of the building. The Hardys hopped out of the van and ran over to Jake.

"Jake, what's going on?" Joe asked.

"They want to take me in for questioning," Jake said. "I didn't do anything. I was just sleeping on the couch when they banged on the door."

"Move back, you two," one of the officers said.

"Jake," Frank said, "don't say anything until they get you a lawyer."

Jake nodded mutely.

"A lawyer can't help this guy," another cop said as he came out of the building. "Not unless he can explain this." He held something up in his hand.

The Hardys could see it was a computer disc with the words "Securitech Master 001" printed on the top. "I found it in his basement storage compartment," the cop said.

"That doesn't belong to me!" Jake said.

"You bet it doesn't," the cop said. "You stole it from Securitech earlier."

118

"I suppose you found the missing computers along with it," Joe said. He crossed his arms over his chest and whispered to Frank, "This stinks. It's a setup!"

"Not yet," the cop replied, "but we will."

"Remember, Jake," Frank said. "Keep mum until you talk with a lawyer. We'll see if our dad can dig one up for you."

Jake nodded again, but this time he looked scared. The police loaded him into one of the squad cars and drove off. The other cops stayed to complete their search.

"Let's go home, Joe," Frank said. "There's nothing more we can do here."

Joe sighed. "Yeah. Let's go. I'm beat."

Neither brother slept much that night. Even after their dad said he'd find a lawyer for Jake, they still couldn't settle down. The confusing facts of the case kept running through their heads until, finally, sleep took them.

They were sitting at the breakfast table on Sunday morning, poking listlessly at their eggs when suddenly a light went on over Joe's head.

"Hey," he said, "I just realized something. Cindy knew we didn't have any evidence against her."

"Well," Frank said glumly, "Con told us as

much." He folded up the newspaper he'd been looking at. It didn't have any new information on the case.

"Yeah," Joe said, "he told *us* as much when he took us aside—but he *didn't* tell her! But she knew it, anyway. She told her mother we didn't have any proof."

Frank snapped his fingers. "You're right!" he said. "And, you know, I bet she knew it even before we took her to the police station? Remember how smug she was in the car?"

Joe nodded. "So, she must have known the system was out. That's why she felt so confident about sabotaging our car. The question is, how did she know?"

"That's easy," Frank said. "She knew because she's in league with whoever pulled the crime. She's in this scheme up to her neck. The question is, who's at the head of the operation?"

"She was wearing a Kings jacket," Joe said. "And we've seen her hanging out with Missy Gates. Seems to me Morelli and his gang are the logical suspects."

"Why don't we pay a visit to the Kings' garage," Frank said.

Thirty minutes later they pulled up a block away from Morelli's house in a rough section of Bayport.

120

The Morelli house had been built in the 1950s and had a brick facade. It had been well maintained despite the neighborhood. The garage next to it was almost larger than the house.

The garage had three car bays and a door. A hand-painted sign above the door read Kings' Repair Service and listed a telephone number.

"Hope they're not upset that we didn't call for an appointment," Joe said.

He and Frank went up to the door. The door had a small window in it, and Joe and Frank peered in.

All the Kings seemed to be present. Vince Morelli, Harley Bettis, Jay Stone, and Missy Gates were all standing at one end of the garage, huddled over a long, well-lit work table. The Hardys could see electronics tools scattered about. The brothers couldn't see what exactly the Kings were looking at.

"Jackpot," Joe whispered. He turned the knob, pushed open the door, and walked in. Frank was right behind him.

A bell rang as they entered, and the Kings turned toward the door. As they did, Frank and Joe could see what they were working on: computers. The computers looked new and top of the line. There were three of them.

Frank glanced at Joe to make sure he and his

brother were thinking the same thing. Joe's expression said they were.

"What do you guys want?" Morelli said. His tone made it clear that the brothers were not welcome.

"They're spying, probably," Missy Gates said.

Harley Bettis sneered. "Let's show them what we do to spies!"

14 Fall Guys

"Back off, Bettis," Joe said. The younger Hardy balled his hands into fists and took a step forward. The other Kings began to pick up tools that were lying around the garage: tire irons, wrenches, chains.

"I wouldn't do that if I were you," Frank said. "Not unless you want to be in even more trouble than you're in now."

"The only one in trouble here," Stone said, "is you punks." He swished his chain in the air.

"That's where you're wrong," Frank said. "If we figured out who had these stolen computers, how far behind do you think the police are?"

"What are you talking about?" Morelli said. "These computers aren't stolen. We bought them."

x

"Maybe so," Joe said. "But the person you bought them from *stole* them from Securitech last night. Don't you guys ever read the paper?"

The Kings looked confused. They relaxed the weapons in their hands and, as one, looked at Missy.

"That's not true!" Missy protested. "Cindy would never—" She cut herself off before saying more, but her words were enough to confirm the Hardys' suspicions.

"Cindy Hamilton's setting you up," Frank said. "At least, that's what *I* think. The police may think otherwise, though. They might think that the Kings are the brains behind the Securitech robbery and the recent vandalism. They may think she's part of your gang."

"Cindy's just a hanger-on," Morelli said. "She's a friend of Missy's. Sometimes we hang out, have fun."

"Does that fun include breaking into Securitech and Councilwoman Hamilton's office?" Joe asked. "If it doesn't, you might want to reconsider letting her hang with you—unless you want *your* neck in the noose."

"Where'd you get those computers?" Frank asked.

"Cindy sold 'em to us," Stone said. "She said her

mom was upgrading their home systems. She'd have thrown them out, otherwise."

"Come on, Stone," Joe said. "You can't be that dumb. Those computers are state of the art."

"Well, they did look expensive," Bettis said. "But if they're so new, why would she have sold them to us so cheap?"

"Because they're hot," Morelli said. "That's why!" He threw his wrench across the garage. It hit a tool chest and clattered to the floor. "How could I have been so stupid!"

"Cindy was counting on your greed," Frank said. "She knew you guys liked to mess around on the Internet as well as fixing cars. She knew you couldn't turn down a deal on decent computers."

"Only trouble is," Joe said, "you didn't know she was setting you up. Good thing we showed up to warn you."

"Well, okay," Morelli said. "You warned us. Now get out of here. We'll take care of Hamilton ourselves."

"That wouldn't be smart, either," Frank said. "She's not in this alone. I don't even think she's the brains of this operation."

"They're right," Missy said. "Cindy couldn't be behind this. I saw some of her college grades last time I went to her house. They were all pretty bad."

125

"Even her computer grades?" Joe asked.

Missy nodded. "Yeah."

"I can believe that," Stone said. "I think she hooked up with that Jake dweeb just so she could get free tutoring."

"She'd need a lot of tutoring to pull off this kind of caper," Joe said.

"But if she's not behind this scam, who is?" Bettis asked.

"We don't know yet," Joe replied.

"But with your help," Frank said, "I think we might be able to catch Cindy and lure the real mastermind into the open. Just give me and Joe a couple of minutes to talk in private and figure this out."

"You're not gonna rat us out to the police, are you?" Bettis asked.

Joe shook his head. "If we wanted to call the cops, we would have done it before we came through that door. Hide the computers if you're worried. Come to think of it, that might be a good idea, anyway."

Joe and Frank stepped outside. "What do you think?" Joe asked.

"It seems pretty clear that the Kings didn't know anything about this," Frank said.

"That's what I think, too. But can we trust them to help us out?"

"If it'll get them off the hook," Frank said, "I think we can."

"I hate to say it," Joe said, "but Jake and Vanessa still look like our best suspects. Cindy has to be working with someone, and either Jake or Vanessa has the computer expertise to pull this off, even if Cindy doesn't."

"Maybe we should check on how good Cindy is with a computer," Frank said.

"How?" Joe asked.

"We could check her school records," Frank said.

"Just walk in and ask for her transcripts?"

"I'm willing to bet that the Kings would hack into the BIT computer to look up her grades if we asked them," Frank said. "It might not be strictly legal, but . . ."

Joe finished the thought for him. "It's a lot better than being caught in the trap Cindy set for them. If she's pulled up her grades, maybe she's the brains after all."

Frank nodded. "Right. You go see if they can do it, I'll use the cell phone in the van to check with Jamal. Maybe he can give us some more information on Vanessa."

"He's been hanging with her enough," Joe said. "He's probably memorized her fingerprints by now."

"I'll be happy if he just knows more about her background than we do," Frank said.

"What about Jake?" Joe asked.

"He'd have to be awfully dumb to plan this caper and then fall asleep on his couch after pulling it off. I don't know that we can rule it out, though."

"You talk to Jamal," Joe said. "I'll talk to the Kings about the grades."

"Check," Frank said. He headed to the van while Joe went back into the garage.

A few minutes later Frank joined his brother and the Kings. "I've got some news about Vanessa," he said. "She's out of the picture."

"How so?" Joe asked. The Kings had hooked up another computer on their workbench and were busy working on it.

"Remember when we left her at work yesterday?"

Joe nodded. "Yeah."

"Well, she got a lift home from Jamal," Frank said. "But instead of going home, they decided to take in a movie. She was with him the whole time the robbery was going on. I called her, and she said she'd do whatever she could to help us track down the real culprits."

"It's good to have her on our side," Joe said. "I'm afraid the news from here isn't so good. Show him, Stoney."

Jay Stone slid away from the computer so Frank could see the screen.

"Cindy's barely passing any of her courses," Stone said, "except for the computer class. At mid-term, it's the only class she's got an A in."

"Looks like that proves she *could* be the brains behind this," Joe said. "She does have the computer know-how. And her access to Jake might have given her the info she needed to break into Securitech."

"They could be in it together," Stone said. "I never did like that Martins dweeb!"

Frank rubbed his chin. "It could mean something else, too," he said.

"What?" Joe asked.

"Just a hunch," Frank said. "I think we should go ahead with our plan to trap Cindy, anyway. I'll fill you in while we set up."

"Great," Joe said. "Morelli's got some videotape equipment upstairs. All we need to do is lure her here."

"I'll do that," Missy said. "I owe her one. A *big* one. She borrowed my jacket yesterday. Looks like she was trying to frame me, too."

"What if we can't get her to confess?" Bettis said.

"I've got an idea about that, too," Frank said. "Let me get Vanessa back on the phone. Maybe, with a little luck, we can get those Securitech cameras to work *for* us rather than against us."

"But there aren't any cameras in this part of town," Joe said.

"That's true, but there are plenty near where her accomplice hangs out," Frank said. "If we plan this right, she'll lead us straight to him."

An hour later all the pieces of the Hardys' plan were in place. Missy had gotten Cindy to agree to come to the Kings' garage. The brothers had set up the Kings' video tape equipment in an old station wagon that Morelli had up on blocks for repair. Frank and Joe had briefed the Kings, and everyone was ready to do his or her part.

After Frank and Joe hid in the back room, all that remained was the waiting. They didn't have to wait long.

Cindy blew into the garage as if she owned it. "What's up?" she asked. "Missy made it sound pretty important on the phone."

The Kings were lounging around near the back workbench. They turned when Cindy came in.

"It's pretty important, all right," Morelli said menacingly.

"Yeah," Bettis agreed, "if you think your future is important."

Cindy looked surprised. "My future? What are you talking about?"

"We know you stole those computers you sold us, Cindy," Stone said.

"Yeah," Missy said. "And unless you pay us to keep quiet, we're going to tell the cops all about it."

15 Caught On Camera

"You guys are crazy," Cindy said. "I don't know what you're talking about." She tried to sound tough, but beads of sweat began to form on her forehead.

Morelli picked up a pair of pliers and threw it across the garage. "You think we don't read the papers, Cindy?" he asked. "You think we couldn't figure out where these computers came from? These are *Securitech's* computers. They're front page news. You made us pay you for them, but instead, you're going to have to pay *us.*"

"Otherwise," Bettis said, "we're going to the cops and telling them everything we know."

Cindy looked around but found no sympathetic faces in the room. "What if you do tell the police? I'm Councilwoman Hamilton's daughter, and you're all just a bunch of thugs. Who are the cops going to believe, me or you?"

"Your prints are on those computers, you know," Missy said.

"Your prints are on those computers, too," Cindy said, brushing a damp lock of hair off her forehead. "All of you."

"Yeah," Stone said, "but what the police will want to know is how *your* prints got there if you didn't sell those computers to us."

"I could say that you made me put my hands on them when you lured me here today," Cindy said, still defiant.

The Kings laughed. Morelli pointed to the camera in the car. "They won't buy that because we've been taping you since the moment you walked through that door."

"Why you—" Cindy said. She made a lunge for the station wagon, but Missy and Bettis cut her off.

"You want that tape," Missy said, "you're going to have to pay for it."

"In cash," Bettis said.

"Fifteen thousand," Stone put in. "Plus the fifteen hundred we gave you for the computers last night."

Cindy's jaw dropped. "I—I don't have that kind of money," she said.

"Maybe you don't," Morelli said, "but your old lady does."

"But I can't get it from *her*," Cindy said. "I've already run up enough bills at college that . . ." She stopped.

"Well," Stone said, "you'd better get it from somewhere, because at seven o'clock sharp that tape is going to the cops."

"But that's only six hours away!" Cindy said, her voice almost pleading now.

Morelli put a toothpick in his mouth and bit it in half. He spit half onto the floor. "You're wasting time then, aren't you?"

Cindy looked at the gang, tears forming in the corners of her eyes. Then she rushed out of the garage, hopped into her SUV, and sped down the street.

Morelli and the Kings looked toward the back room where Frank and Joe were still hiding.

"What now?" Morelli asked.

Frank and Joe stepped into the garage. "Now," Joe said, "we spring the trap."

Frank had the cell phone to his ear and was talking into it. "Yeah. She just left. Great. I know you can't see her now, but if you keep an eye on the campus area, I'm sure she'll show up soon. Right. We'll keep the line open."

"What are you guys going to do?" Stone asked.

"We're going to follow her to her accomplice," Joe said.

"I've got a friend of ours on the line," Frank said. "She got her boss at Securitech to agree to lend us a hand. We'll take it from here."

"What about us?" Missy asked.

"You call the police and give them that tape," Joe said.

"It doesn't seem right, somehow," Bettis said, "turning the tape in to the cops. Maybe we could still make some dough with it."

"And maybe you could end up in jail as an accomplice after the fact or a blackmailer," Joe said.

"Don't forget to turn in the computers, too," Frank added.

"Hey!" Morelli said. "We paid good money for those computers."

"You'll probably get some kind of reward," Joe said. "Besides, I'm sure you'll get the money back from Cindy, one way or another."

"And think of how it'll make Councilwoman Hamilton squirm," Frank said.

That brought a smile to the Kings' faces. "Hey," Stone said, "this could be good. We'd almost be, like, *heroes.*"

Frank and Joe smiled. "Not a bad payoff, in the end."

"Yeah, okay," Morelli said. "Good luck catching Cindy's pal—whoever he may be."

"I think we've got a pretty good idea," Frank said. He and Joe headed for their van.

As Joe got behind the wheel, he asked, "Is Vanessa still on the line?"

Frank nodded. "Yeah. And she's hooked into the Securitech system. Clark Kubrick was only too happy to help out once she explained our theory to him."

"Let's just hope your theory pans out," Joe said. "If it doesn't, Jake is in deep trouble."

"Either way," Frank said, "it should lead us to the real culprit. I'd be sad if the criminal turned out to be Jake, but we've got to catch whoever is behind all this."

Joe nodded and headed for the campus area.

"You still there, Vanessa?" Frank asked into the phone. "I'm going to put you on the speaker so Joe can hear, too."

"I'm here," Vanessa said. "And it looks like you guys were right. The cameras picked up Cindy a couple of minutes ago, and it looks like she's heading straight for the campus. She'll be lucky if she's not stopped by the police, the way she's driving."

"Let's hope *that* doesn't happen," Joe said. "That would ruin everything. Are the cops there with you?"

"Con Riley is," Vanessa said. "He says they've got another car out on the street, too, tailing her."

"Well, ask him if he can call off the other prowl cars," Frank said, "to make sure she doesn't get stopped for speeding before she gets where she's going."

Vanessa said something unintelligible to Con, then, to the Hardys, she said, "I told him. He said he'd see what he could do."

"How far behind her are we?" Joe asked.

"About five minutes," Vanessa said. "She just got caught in some lights downtown. You can save a few minutes by cutting up Keel Street and avoiding the jam."

"Thanks," Joe said. "You're better than an onboard computer."

"I try," Vanessa said. The speaker fell silent for a few moments. Then Vanessa added, "She's on Smith now, moving toward the campus."

"I'm just turning on to Smith," Joe said.

"We see you," Vanessa said. "She's only a couple of minutes ahead of you now."

"We're coming up on the moment of truth," Frank said.

Joe nodded. They waited for a few minutes in tense silence. Joe gripped the wheel tightly.

Finally, Vanessa said, "She's turned off! She's on Oberlin Avenue now!"

Frank and Joe let out a long sigh of relief. "Looks like that puts Jake in the clear," Frank said.

"Thank goodness!" Vanessa said over the speaker.

"I bet Kubrick's disappointed," Joe said.

Vanessa laughed. "Not really. But he is surprised. I think I just heard his jaw hit the floor."

"This has to be the strangest car chase I've ever been in," Joe said.

"She's stopped," Vanessa said. "You should be able to see her across the quadrangle."

Frank looked out the window. "Got her!" he said. "Come on, Joe, we can't lose her now."

"We don't want her to see us, though," Joe said. He pulled the car around the block and parked out of sight of Cindy's car.

"She's walking up to the house," Vanessa said.

"We're coming at the house from her blind side," Frank said. "Tell Con to have his men come a-running. And tell them to bring that search warrant." He flipped the phone shut and stuck it in his pocket.

The house was large and built in the Victorian style. The property had been well kept up—the bushes were trimmed and the lawn carefully mowed. Frank and Joe moved quietly down the sidewalk, taking care not to be seen.

As they approached the corner of the house, they could hear voices from the front steps. One of the voices was Cindy's. She sounded frantic.

138

"You don't understand!" she said. "We're caught!"

"You mean *you're* caught," a man's voice corrected her. "And you wouldn't have been if you had done as I instructed. You should have dumped those computers, not sold them!"

"I needed the money," Cindy said.

"Money, money. That's all you students ever think about," the man said. "If you weren't so greedy, you wouldn't be in trouble. Raise the money if you like. You won't get it from me. Neither you, nor the police, can connect me to this crime."

Joe and Frank stepped around the corner.

Joe looked at Cindy and the man standing on the doorstep in front of her. He smiled and said, "I wouldn't be too sure about that, Professor Firestein."

16 Smile!

"What are you doing here?" Firestein demanded, his face crimson.

"We knew Cindy had an accomplice in the Securitech robbery," Joe said, "but at first we couldn't figure out who it was."

"Then we discovered that she was almost flunking out of college," Frank said. "In fact, the only class she was passing with flying colors was yours, professor."

"That means nothing," Firestein said. "Cindy is a fine student. And I don't know what you're talking about. What Securitech robbery?"

"The one you engineered," Joe said. "Cindy was with us when it happened. So she couldn't have pulled it off by herself. She had to be working with someone."

"Odds were, whoever she was working with was the brains behind the operation," Frank said.

"I don't know what you're talking about, either," Cindy said. "When my mother finds out you two are harassing me again . . ."

Joe tapped his temple with two fingers. "See," he said, "not too bright. She hasn't figured out that she's been caught, even though the Kings videotaped her confessing her part in the crime not half an hour ago."

At the word "videotaped" the professor's jaw dropped. He looked at a nearby light pole and spotted the Securitech camera mounted there. Panic spread across his face.

"Smile," Frank said. "You're on Securitech camera."

The brothers grinned, and looked up the street toward the arriving police car.

Two hours later the Hardys were relaxing at the police station with Officer Con Riley.

"Well," Con said as he settled into the seat behind his desk, "you were right. We turned up a CDR copy of the Securitech master disc in the professor's house, along with some papers that led us to believe that he was moonlighting for a rival high-tech security firm. He was going to sell the code on that disc for a lot of money. How did you guys figure it out?"

141

"It was the only thing that made sense," Frank said. "Obviously, the computers had been stolen for the control disc. That's why the disc turned up in Jake's storage area and the computers in a different place entirely."

"Firestein was smart enough to figure out that Securitech would tumble to the real object of the theft quickly," Joe said. "The computers were just a smoke screen, as was the rest of the vandalism, for that matter. What Firestein didn't know was that his accomplice would get greedy and try to sell the computers rather than dump them. If Cindy had done as he instructed, I don't know that we'd ever have caught either of them."

Con nodded. "It was a clever plan. Tell me, though, how did Firestein close down the Securitech system? I could understand how it might be possible *after* he stole the disc—but he did it *before* the break-in. He couldn't have gotten past their internal security or the cameras otherwise."

"That was one of the trickiest parts of this setup," Joe said. "He was using his students—a number of whom also worked for Securitech, like Jake and, earlier, Vanessa—and picking their brains."

Frank nodded. "He knew a bit about how the Securitech system was supposed to work, so he gave assignments to his class that would give him enough information to work out the rest. It took longer than he'd hoped because Vanessa dropped out rather than violate her confidentiality agreement with Securitech."

"She caught on a lot faster than Jake did," Joe said. "Though, of course, she didn't suspect Firestein's real motive. After she dropped out, he really turned up the heat on Jake."

"We're not sure exactly when Cindy came into the picture," Frank said. "Maybe Firestein chose her for his accomplice because she was Jake's girlfriend for a while—or maybe it was because she had such bad grades and he knew he could tempt her into breaking the law for a passing mark."

"In any case," Joe said, "she did a lot of his dirty work."

"But she didn't do the Securitech break-in," Con said.

"No," Frank replied. "She was with us at the police station when it happened. That really threw us for a while. We had been pretty convinced that she was behind the break-ins and the vandalism."

"And she was, most of the time," Joe said. "We think that the first time the Securitech system went off it was just a dry run for Firestein. He wanted to make sure his plan would work, so he turned the system off for a few minutes and sent Cindy out to cause some chaos—just to see if she'd be caught."

"So, she chose her mother's office to vandalize," Con said.

Joe and Frank nodded.

"Boy," Con said, leaning back in his chair, "I wonder what went wrong in *that* family."

"Who knows?" Frank said.

"Personally, I think Cindy's just a bad egg," Joe said. "I mean, look at the way she bopped poor Jake on the head. There was no need for that; she's just mean."

"She went after you two as well," Con said.

Frank nodded. "Good thing, too. If she'd stuck to the plan, we might not have figured it out and Jake might be rotting in a cell somewhere."

"When she was trying to let the air out of our tires, she was waiting for Firestein," Joe said. "He had time to break in to Securitech, but for his plan to work, he needed someone else to tidy up. So, we figure he stashed the computers in her car near the scene."

"That way, if anyone stopped him for any reason, they wouldn't find anything on him," Frank said. "All he had to hide was one small computer disc. Then, while Cindy was supposed to dump the computers, Firestein was copying the disc."

"Then he went to Jake's apartment—which isn't covered by Securitech cameras, and planted the disc in Jake's storage locker," Joe said. "Jake was his fall guy because the police had to catch someone for the crime. If they didn't, Securitech would figure out that their code had been pirated a lot more quickly than they would have otherwise. But with the disc recovered so soon after the robbery, they'd relax, and Firestein could go about his dirty business."

"We found a key to Jake's apartment on Cindy's key ring when we arrested her," Con said.

"That makes sense," Frank said. "She must have gotten it from him when they were dating. And it probably explains what Cindy dropped the first time we met her—in the darkened hall outside Jake's apartment—those keys. Probably Firestein got a copy from her as well so he could frame Jake."

"Professor Firestein was pretty desperate to get the code at that point, I'd guess," Joe said. "He needed it fast because he knew that the system would be easiest to break into the first few days it was running. No one expects a computer system to work perfectly right away, so his tampering would be more difficult to detect."

"Whether Cindy went to the apartment to pressure Jake or to try to steal some computer code for Firestein because Jake was behind in his assignment, we can't say," Frank said. "Either way, both of them nearly got away with it."

Con sat up and took a sip of his coffee. "Well, I'm just glad you Hardys were on the case," he said. "I'm not saying that the police wouldn't have figured it out eventually—we cops are not as dumb as you think—but . . ."

"I'm just glad that we caught the real criminals and cleared Jake," Joe said.

Frank yawned. "I think, at this point, we've earned some well-deserved rest."

He and Joe got up and headed toward the door. "See you soon, Officer Riley."

Con Riley leaned back in his chair and scratched his head.

On Monday evening the Hardys and their parents decided to eat out. The brothers chose Java John's, and the four of them met Jamal, Vanessa, and Jake there, too.

"Let me get this right," Jake said. "Professor Firestein was using me to steal Securitech's computer code so he could control their security system. Then he broke into the company, stole their master disc, and planted it in my storage locker, to make it look like I'd done it."

"Right," Joe and Frank said simultaneously.

"And Cindy was in on it," Jake said, shaking his head. "Man, that's hard to take. I think I feel my headache coming back. She hit me with those bottles, too?"

"Let's face it, Jake," Vanessa said, smiling, "you have no taste in women."

"That must be why you're my friend," Jake said.

The Hardys, Jamal, and Vanessa all laughed. Even Jake smiled a bit.

"You'll all be happy to know," Fenton Hardy said, "that Mrs. Hardy and I have spent a lot of time on the phone today."

"We've talked to a lot of politicians," Laura Hardy said, "and they assured us that the Securitech system will be turned off—at least until the city has time to rethink its position."

Fenton took a sip of water and said, "Despite catching some criminals—and despite the clever use our sons put it to—the Securitech system was obviously very vulnerable to abuse."

"Well, I'm pretty tired of being an unwitting TV star," Frank said.

"Fifteen minutes of fame enough for you, Frank?" Jamal asked.

"More than enough," Frank replied. "What about you, Joe?"

"I'll be more than happy to see Big Brother closed down for good," Joe said. "After all, cameras may not lie—but sometimes they don't tell the whole truth, either."

**Do your younger brothers and sisters
want to read books like yours?**

**Let them know there
are books just for *them!***

They can join Nancy Drew and her best
friends as they collect clues and solve
mysteries in

THE

NANCY DREW

NOTEBOOKS®

Starting with

#1 The Slumber Party Secret

#2 The Lost Locket

#3 The Secret Santa

#4 Bad Day for Ballet

AND

**Meet up with suspense and mystery
in The Hardy Boys® are: The Clues Brothers™**

Starting with

#1 The Gross Ghost Mystery

#2 The Karate Clue

#3 First Day, Worst Day

#4 Jump Shot Detectives

Published by Pocket Books

BILL WALLACE

Award-winning author Bill Wallace brings you fun-filled
animal stories full of humor and exciting adventures.

BEAUTY

RED DOG*

TRAPPED IN DEATH CAVE*

A DOG CALLED KITTY

DANGER ON PANTHER PEAK

SNOT STEW

**FERRET IN THE BEDROOM,
LIZARDS IN THE FRIDGE**

DANGER IN QUICKSAND SWAMP

THE CHRISTMAS SPURS

TOTALLY DISGUSTING!

BUFFALO GAL

NEVER SAY QUIT

BIGGEST KLUTZ IN FIFTH GRADE

BLACKWATER SWAMP

WATCHDOG AND THE COYOTES

TRUE FRIENDS

JOURNEY INTO TERROR

THE FINAL FREEDOM

THE BACKWARD BIRD DOG

UPCHUCK AND THE ROTTEN WILLY

**UPCHUCK AND THE ROTTEN WILLY:
THE GREAT ESCAPE**

THE FLYING FLEA, CALLIE, AND ME

ALOHA SUMMER

**UPCHUCK AND THE ROTTEN WILLY:
RUNNING WILD**

 A MINSTREL® BOOK
Published by Pocket Books

The Fascinating Story of One of the World's Most Celebrated Naturalists

Celebrating 40 years with the wild chimpanzees

MY LIFE with the
CHIMPANZEES

by JANE GOODALL

From the time she was girl, Jane Goodall dreamed of a life spent working with animals. Finally, when she was twenty-six years old, she ventured into the forests of Africa to observe chimpanzees in the wild. On her expeditions she braved the dangers of the jungle and survived encounters with leopards and lions in the African bush. And she got to know an amazing group of wild chimpanzees—intelligent animals whose lives bear a surprising resemblance to our own.

Illustrated with photographs

A Byron Preiss Visual Publications, Inc. Book

🐾 A Minstrel® Book
Published by Pocket Books

Todd Strasser's
AGAINST THE ODDS ™

Shark Bite
The sailboat is sinking, and Ian just saw the
biggest shark of his life.

Grizzly Attack
They're trapped in the Alaskan wilderness
with no way out.

Buzzard's Feast
Danger in the desert!

Gator Prey
They know the gators are coming for
them...it's only a matter of time.

A MINSTREL® BOOK
Published by Pocket Books   2023